THE KILLING MACHINE

For all my high-tech friends.

Revenge

Chapter 1

Tempest thought the worst day of his life was over. Although he was the top engineer at work, assigned to special projects because of his security level, funding had been pulled and the project died with it, totally shut down. He was no longer needed. There was no room for rebuttal. His desk had been cleaned out while he was at lunch, and he was escorted out of the building by two security cops he had never met.

Had that not been enough, he drove to the gym, something his wife Amy had suggested years before, and overexerted himself on the StairMaster, had a not-too-nutritious snack, and pined privately over his misfortune, then hit the StairMaster again until his early evening Tae Kwon Do class. He would have cried, but that didn't suit him. Exhaustion and thought were much more important. He knew he'd come up with an idea; he just needed to let go of the initial shock of what happened, and over-exercising would help him do that. By the time his Tae Kwon Do class started though, he felt so tired, he didn't perform well at all.

He didn't want to tell Amy any sooner than he had to, but when he returned to his locker, he saw she had texted him several times because he wasn't at work.

I HEARD, one text said simply.

WHERE ARE YOU? ARE YOU ALL RIGHT?

He wasn't. After all, they had just bought a new house once they found she was pregnant—about which they were both hugely excited—and unemployment wasn't what they needed at the moment.

But he didn't want her to worry, so he called. "I'm sorry, Amy. I just had to be alone for a little while."

"You don't have to apologize about being alone, Ten. I know you. I was just worried." There was a short silence. "I have an idea."

"Will it get my job back?"

"Russell called." Her voice purred in his ear. "It's his birthday and he wants to meet at Goldie's. He sounded desperate. Like you were his only friend. I told him I'd let you know once I heard from you. Why don't you have a drink, whine about your day to get it off your chest, and come home later in a better mood."

"I love you."

"I'll let him know you said yes. I'll see you later."

He heard her hang up. What a woman. He had never met anyone who understood him better. He showered and left the gym, got into his Camry, and pulled out of the lot. Another car almost sideswiped him even though the driver was looking straight at him. Thank goodness for his reflexes. On the way to Goldie's, the streets felt more dangerous after his close call. He even had to speed up to stop from getting T-boned at another intersection, which put him on high alert. Goldie's wasn't far from his house; maybe he should leave the car parked in their lot overnight. After all, he'd read that most accidents happen within a few miles of home.

Ten locked the Camry and wandered into the bar. The place was louder and busier than he'd ever seen it. A television in the corner displayed news, but the sound was off. He saw Russell hunched over the bar with an empty seat next to him. He didn't look like he was in a birthday mood. Ten walked over and reached for Russell's shoulder, but his friend swung around and slapped his hand away, then stared at him.

"You okay?"

"Sorry." Russell glanced around the room. He got off his stool and hugged Ten. "I don't like this place being so busy."

"I thought it was your birthday. I didn't even know—"

"It's not my birthday." He scanned the room again.

"What's going on?"

"There's not much time to explain everything. But it's about your work, your project."

Ten lowered his eyes. "I was laid off today."

"No, Ten, you finished the project. That's why they let you go. That's all that was supposed to happen too. But that decision changed a few hours later." He turned his head away, looked around nervously, and brought his attention back to Ten. "I'm part of a team, a group called ISTI. International Security for Technological Innovations." He shook his head as though it didn't matter. "I've been with them for nearly twenty years, been assigned to you for the last seven."

"Assigned to me?"

"A bodyguard, so to speak. Protection. But I have to tell you, I didn't buy into this. Not killing our own." He shook his head.

Ten scrunched up his face. "What are you talking about?"

"It's one thing to pull a project, another thing to kill everyone involved. Trust me. I'm not alone on this. Other bodyguards feel the same about their assignments."

"Bodyguard? Project? What's happening? You still haven't told me."

Russell placed a hand on Ten's shoulder. "Divide and conquer. Six scientists, six pieces of one puzzle. I don't know what the project is, none of us do. We can only guess. But I know it's over. They want me to take you out. So, I'm telling you: disappear. You don't have much time."

Ten's head floated full of information, pieces of information. He didn't know what to do, what to ask. "I'm not following this. Are you for real? All this? I mean, I've gone along this far, but..." Russell's expression shifted, more stern, more believable. "Okay, how much time do I have?" It was the only thing Ten could think to ask.

"Don't know. Look, they don't know I'm refusing. They think I'm still looking for you, after you disappeared from work."

"I was escorted out. I went to the gym."

Russell smiled. "I didn't think of that." A lie he must have told his superiors. "Look, I've got to check in soon. I'll be in touch when I can. I'll do everything to steer them clear of you and Amy."

"Amy?"

"Get home and get out." He patted Ten's shoulder. "I'll hold them off as long as I can. If they knew I was talking with you like this..." He glanced around the room again. From his pocket, he pulled a folded sheet of paper. "They're after everyone on the project. I know they are. And anyone else who might know something." His mouth pulled into a tight grimace. "I'm sure I'll be on the kill list eventually."

"You're scaring me, Russell."

Russell shoved the folded paper into Ten's shirt pocket. "The names of the people responsible for making this decision. Plus the other scientists involved. Hide this. Memorize it. Warn the others." He shoved away from Ten. "We can't be seen together for now. We'll have to meet somewhere. Pack up. Bring Amy and the dog." He looked at his watch and shook his head. "Two hours. Can you do that? Meet me at Casey's Restaurant, in the parking lot. I'll come up with a plan. Now go." Russell turned and rushed out the rear door of the bar.

Ten paused. Why was Russell in such a hurry to get out of there? He tried to pull everything together into some kind of coherent whole. Russell sounded scared. He'd rushed away as though Ten, or he, were being watched, as though they were in danger or something. He patted the paper in his pocket, but instead of looking at it, he made his way toward the rear door only a few minutes after Russell. He wanted more information from his friend.

As Ten opened the door, a blast of light and heat slammed him back against the closing door. He instinctively bent down and covered his head. Flames rolled from Russell's car. The blast caused Ten's ears to ring, the intense heat burned the hairs on his arm. The explosion still resonated in the air.

At the moment, he couldn't think straight. It must have been a car bomb. Russell was dead. He lost his job. Amy! Russell said to pack up. He had to get home.

He ran back into the bar as other patrons forced their way toward the back door where the noise had come from. Ten pushed through the mob and headed into the front lot. Barely out the door, he noticed someone stand up next to his car, as though he had just been looking under the frame. All Ten could think was that there was another bomb being planted, and he turned away as though it wasn't his car.

He lowered his eyes and walked around the corner of the bar. He ran into another man, who swung at him. Ten stepped back and the man missed. He was big, with broad shoulders and dark hair. Dressed in a suit. Ten had stepped into a fighting stance, his hands in the standard, flat, knife-hand position. When the man swung again, Ten blocked using his elbow, then stepped back again rather than advancing. The other man made a shallow laugh at Ten. "Fancy," he said. Then he stepped forward and swung a third time.

Ten blocked again with his elbow, turned into the man's body, thrust his elbow into the big man's abdomen, then brought a fist to his nose. He stepped aside and hit the back of the man's head with his elbow and the man went down. He had never done anything like that before—full contact. He knew the moves and the theory of how to knock a man out—or even kill him—but that was not part of his practice in class.

The man lay on the ground. Ten glanced up and no one appeared to have noticed. His heart beat fast. He stepped aside, took a deep breath, and jogged away from the bar, then jumped a short chain-link fence, and ran toward a strip mall. He continued past the mall lot and into a small grove of trees that eventually opened into the housing development where he and Amy lived. It was the fastest route. The sun had already dropped from view, but an auburn haze held in the air. It would be dark soon. The woods were already darker than the mall parking lot. He stopped long enough to notice that he wasn't being followed. Whoever *they* were, they probably figured he'd just get in his car and be blown to bits, even after what happened to Russell.

Ten caught his breath and ran the rest of the way to the edge of the development. From there, he heard another explosion—ahead of him. A ball of light burst into the air right near where his house should have been, and he knew that's what it was. "Oh my God." He took off toward the explosion. Sweat dripped from his head and down his cheeks. He heard the sound of his own footfalls and wished he were more silent so he could hear if anyone followed him. He touched his shirt pocket with the folded paper inside. Now more than ever, he wanted to look at that list. But he couldn't stop running; he couldn't look until he knew if it was his house that had burst into flames.

And when he turned around a bend, there it was. The house blazed in the early evening sky. His dog, Groucho, barked at something in the back yard. Ten couldn't search for him though. Not now. He ran up and unlocked the front door, traveled through a living room on fire, and ran up the stairs, screaming, "Amy! Amy!"

He held his arms up against the flames, running up the hall wall, one of the main supports for the house, which would eventually collapse around him. Amy lay on the bed in the bedroom, a pillow over her head. He ripped it away and knelt beside her and took her into his arms and kissed her mouth, her cheek. Another explosion happened somewhere downstairs. Groucho's barking continued out back. Ten felt for Amy's pulse. She had been smothered. Tears joined the salty sweat of his cheeks. The heat became worse as one of the bedroom walls split open with flames.

Ten knelt next to Amy in tears. He held her hand against his cheek and kissed her fingers. The heat intensified. His hands shook. His eyes blurred with sweat and tears. But somehow his mind cleared and his actions became more methodical, like he knew automatically what to do next.

Out the window, he saw a man approach Groucho. Groucho lunged at the man to bite him, ever the protective animal, but the man leapt back, removed a pistol from under his arm, and shot the dog. Ten fell to the floor. His chest wanted to explode. His eyes blew out more tears. He shook his head. What was happening? What was he supposed to do? Why were they after him? He finished dressing, took the time to tie his tennis shoes, and grabbed a backpack from under the bed. He heard a window break downstairs. When he looked outside, he noticed the man must have thrown Groucho's body through a window into the house.

Before he left—flames had engulfed the inside wall of the bedroom—he retrieved his wallet, cell phone, and the list Russell had given him. Ten ran into the blazing hall, through flames, and leapt over the banister into the living room, which was equally aflame. He landed so hard that, at first, he thought he'd broken his ankle, but it was merely pain, not a break. He saw Groucho lying on the floor and knelt next to him, reached out, and petted his fur. Then he ducked into the kitchen and grabbed a knife from the rack. He pulled fruit from a bowl on the counter and stuffed it into his backpack, then went out the back door. The grill had blown to bits. That must have been the second explosion. He ran as hard as he could toward the woods on the opposite side of the development. When he stopped, he heard other footsteps and knew he was being followed.

Chapter 2

In the dark, Ten took a few steps near a tree where he felt safer, hidden. He could barely see at first, then his eyes adjusted. His ears pricked, too, as he listened to the soft sound of someone walking toward him. Whoever it was, they couldn't see any better than he could. The steps halted, then moved again. Ten shifted his weight and a twig snapped under him. The footsteps of the other person came faster. When they were close, Ten stepped out and took a hit to the jaw, which knocked him to the side. The man threw another punch at Ten's mid-section. He wasn't ready for the punches, wasn't in a stance. The man hit him again.

Ten was on his knees and the man began to reach under his arm. Again, Ten's mind cleared and he rammed his head into the man's groin, then stood, ramming the top of his head into the man's jaw; he went down. Ten reached inside the man's coat and found the pistol and pulled it out. He had never used one before, but knew the basic premise. He looked for a safety and disengaged it. He turned toward the man and pointed the gun, but couldn't shoot him. He dropped down and reached into the man's pockets and removed his car keys and stuffed them inside his backpack along with the pistol.

He swung around and ran back toward his house. If the man operated alone, then there'd be a car nearby. If he wasn't alone, then… Ten decided not to step into the open.

He heard sirens and the loud horn of the fire trucks coming. He rushed around the side of his neighbor's house. Everyone was outside heading toward the fire. Ten pulled the keys from his pocket. The hit man wouldn't leave his car nearby, so Ten wandered a street over and started to push the unlock button on the man's key fob. He continued to the next street and, about halfway down the block, heard the car beep and saw the lights flash. He ran for the car, opened the door, and jumped inside.

"Who are you?"

Ten looked over. A young girl sat next to him. She didn't look particularly scared. "Friend of your dad's," he said.

"Is he coming?"

Ten started the car, pushed the lock button next to the door, and pulled into the street. "No. I knocked him out. He's in the woods." Ten turned toward the girl, who leaned against the door away from him. "Your dad killed my wife and dog."

"I heard the explosion—"

"He blew up my house."

The girl shook her head and made a face. She looked to be high school age.

Ten asked, "What's your name?"

"Renda Parke," she said.

"That your dad's name? Parke?"

"No. He's my stepdad. Torry Esposito."

"Jesus. The mob."

"What's your name?" she asked.

"Tempest, but everyone calls me Ten."

"Tem?"

"No, Ten, like the number. It stands for Tempest Eugene Nesbit. There, now you know enough about me to get me killed."

"You've pushed that button yourself," she said. "So where are you taking me?"

"Away for now, until I can think."

"Why would anyone want to kill your wife and dog?"

Ten turned onto 495, heading north toward Boston. "Some project I was working on. I'm not sure really."

"What do you do?"

"I'm an engineer, bioengineering."

"If you're smart enough to be an engineer, you're smart enough to figure this out."

Ten had to laugh. "A bit precocious, aren't you?"

She didn't say anything. He kept driving. In a moment, her cell phone rang. She reached to the floor of the car for her purse.

"Hold it."

She kept reaching and Ten shoved her back against the seat with his arm.

"What are you doing?" she yelled at him.

"You're not answering that. Let it go to voicemail."

She cocked her head. "I know what my dad does. You must have done something wrong."

"I'm an engineer on a top-secret project. Nothing wrong in that."

"Weapons?"

"No."

"Come on, you must know."

Ten reached over and unzipped his backpack enough to shove his hand inside and pull out the pistol. "Shut up and sit quietly so I can think."

"That's my dad's gun."

"And you wouldn't want to be shot by your dad's gun. You'd be dead and he'd go to prison."

"Not with your prints on it."

Ten looked her square in the eye. "I know how to clean one of these up."

She crossed her arms and sat with her back against the door.

Ten didn't know what he was going to do with her. He couldn't just leave her, and she didn't look old enough to drive. What he did know was they'd be after her dad's car soon enough. He had to ditch it. He pulled off the highway when he saw a sign with several fast-food restaurants advertised. There was a gas station with a convenience store. He put the gun back into the backpack.

"You're coming with me. If you make one peep, I swear I'll take this gun out and shoot you. My life's on the line here. I have nothing to lose."

She nodded.

He got out and went to her side of the car to open the door. She slid out and walked beside him. Inside the store, he grabbed scissors, a razor, cheap hair dye, a few power bars, a couple bottles of water. "You want anything?"

She gave him a funny look. "No."

At the counter, the guy pointed at a small television he was watching. "You look like that guy that died in a fire tonight."

"That was a woman," Ten said.

The attendant shook his head. "Whole family. Husband, wife, dog. Something exploded."

"Well, I'm not him."

"Obviously, man." The attendant laughed. "You're not going to dye your daughter's hair are you?" He held up the dye.

Ten looked over at Renda. "Her friends are coming over."

She smiled.

"That's $47.27."

Ten paid with cash. "There a bank machine here?"

"Next to the door as you leave," the attendant said.

Ten stopped and withdrew five hundred in cash, his limit. He'd do the same again tomorrow and the next day, until they closed him out. Once outside, he glanced around. A McDonald's sat across the street with a parking lot filled with cars. "Come on."

"Now what?"

He grabbed her wrist and dragged her across the street. "You'd better start to cooperate or your dad can pick you up at the morgue."

"You won't hurt me. You're not like that."

Ten dragged her behind a bush and backhanded her. It hurt him to do so, but he had no choice. He didn't know what else to do. He had to somehow show her that he meant what he said.

She started to cry.

"Your dad killed my wife. I will kill you," he said. Something inside him knew he didn't mean it, but something else inside him told him that he could do it if he had to. He let those two ideas argue it out while he grabbed her wrist again and pulled her near the rear of the lot. He found a car with the window partway down and told her to shove her arm through and to push the unlock button.

She did what he asked.

"Inside." He shoved her and she climbed over the console to the passenger seat while he knelt next to the car and hotwired it.

"How do you know how to do that?"

"I'm an engineer, remember? I know a lot of tricks." He backed out and drove heading toward the highway again.

"They'll just call it in as stolen," she said. "You probably have about ten minutes."

"Don't need that long," he said. He looked over at her. "Did I hurt you?"

She touched her cheek. "Nothing that hasn't happened before."

"Sorry to hear that."

Two exits closer to Boston and Ten took an exit where he found a cheap hotel. He passed it, drove the car off the road and into the back parking lot of a strip mall. Then he dragged Renda to the hotel, threatened her as before, and paid for a room. They walked up the stairs to an outside door. She never tried to get away and walked with him as though they were friends. He opened the door to the room and shoved her inside.

"Nice," she said sarcastically.

The room had one bed and a desk with a single chair in front of it. A dresser against one wall held an old television set. "Good enough for what we need."

"How much time do you think you have?"

Ten removed the gun from his backpack and pointed it at Renda. "You're cutting and dyeing my hair." He removed his shirt.

"You're pretty buff for an engineer."

"I work out." He waved the gun at her. "Let's go."

She followed him into the bathroom where Ten stepped into the tub.

"You going to let me go then?" she asked.

"We'll see."

Chapter 3

Ten looked in the mirror over the sink. He hardly looked like himself, the person staring back at him, and all he had done was cut his hair and change its color. He held the gun in his left hand while he shaved with his other hand. He left the beginnings of a mustache and shaved the rest. He left his sideburns longer, too, figuring that he'd look like some hick once they grew in better. If he had that much time.

Renda sat on the edge of the tub. She crossed her arms. "We done?"

"Thanks for the help," he said.

"You'll need it."

"You don't have to tell me. Enough has already happened."

"I'm sorry about that. I really am." She looked sorry. "That brown hair color looks awful on you."

"That's the idea for now." He grabbed his things, walked into the other room, and threw everything into his backpack again, waving the pistol at Renda the whole time so she'd follow him. "You can sit at the desk."

She plopped down. "Now what?"

He took a deep breath and looked at his watch. It was 11:30 p.m. He wanted to sleep. "We wait for a half hour, then steal another car." Ten waved the gun around again. "These people will be tucked in by then. The missing car won't get noticed until morning. Gives us plenty of time."

He pulled the paper Russell had given him from his pocket and unfolded it with one hand.

"You can put that down. I'm not going to run away."

Ten sat on the floor in front of the door with his backpack beside him. He placed the gun on the floor.

Renda huffed as though what he did was unnecessary, but she didn't say anything more.

There were two rows of names side-by-side written in ink on the paper. One was labeled Team, while the other was labeled Decision Makers. He noticed that the first name on the Decision Maker list was his immediate supervisor, who he never really got along with very well. In Ten's mind, Griffin Bower was a pompous ass who appeared to do little work, bragged about his boat all the time, and hammered everyone else about deadlines.

There were six names on each list, and he wondered if that was just coincidence. He recognized all the names on the Team list, and all but two on the Decision Maker list. Several names on the Team consisted of scientists he'd either worked with directly or communicated with through project notes back and forth. These people were located all over the US. Maria Tanner's name was there. She worked with Bailey & Bradshaw Pharmaceuticals in Michigan. She had signed off on a few of his circuit drawings, and they had talked several times over the phone. She worked in bioelectronic technology, so they had a lot in common. Sharon Pontrelli was on the list too. He knew the name but was surprised to see it. Sharon was a highly regarded chemist working on disease control. She had won a Pulitzer for her DNA research on switching cancer cells off and on using nanobots. Was that what he was involved with? Disease control? It made sense. Until now, Ten would never have guessed she was involved in the same project he worked on.

The Decision Makers included Griffin, Ten's supervisor at the NanoTech Division of Pi Industries; a senator from California, Scott Cornhill; Dryden Smithers,

CEO of Smithers Pharmaceuticals; Eric Webber, who sat on the president's cabinet as Secretary of Technological Innovations; and two other men he didn't recognize: Jacob Metzger and Jasper Ignato. He refolded the list. He would let the names percolate in his mind while he stayed safe.

Ten opened the box of ziplock bags and pulled one out, then dropped the list into the bag and zipped it shut before putting it back into his shirt pocket.

"Figure it out yet?" Renda asked.

"I will," he said.

"I believe you. That is, if you live long enough."

"I don't care."

"You must if you're still fighting," she said.

"Well, I don't. But as long as I'm alive, I'll work on figuring this out, and on killing those responsible for Amy's death."

"That your wife?"

"She was pregnant." Ten stared at the floor. He didn't want to look into the innocent face of Renda Parke. He didn't want to see her brown eyes staring back at him. He wished she weren't even there, but he needed her at the moment.

"That's terrible." She sounded sincere.

He shook his head.

"But you didn't kill my dad. Maybe you can't do it."

"I want the decision makers," he said. "People always punish the workers, the doers; they never go after the source. I want the source to feel what their decisions mean. They think they're off the hook because they hire someone else to do the dirty work. No, I want the decision makers."

"I believe you."

Ten didn't say anything.

After sitting in silence for a few minutes, they heard a few people talking outside their door. Men's voices. Ten raised his palm to keep Renda quiet. Someone knocked on their door

"Shit." He waved the gun for her to come to him. "Get up," he whispered. He held her in front of him. "Who is it?"

"Give us the girl." The man didn't waste any time.

Ten shook his head. "Not on your life," he said quietly to Renda.

Another knock. "We're comin' in, cowboy."

The lock turned, then the doorknob. As the door started to open, Ten shoved Renda onto the bed. He saw someone's arm and shoulder enter the room and fear took over. He realized he could die right there. He kicked the door as hard as possible. It slammed onto the man's arm. There was a loud crack and a moan. Ten's heart raced and his instincts took over. He grabbed the knob and threw the door open, swung the butt of the gun across the first man's head, then raised the pistol and shot the other man in the face before he realized what he'd done.

He fell backward.

Renda screamed.

Ten bent to the floor and coughed. He thought he was going to vomit but didn't. He reached for Renda, pulled her in front of him, and walked out the door onto the walkway. He stepped around the man he'd knocked out and over the dead man. He held the gun pointed at Renda's head. His hand shook uncontrollably. Over the railing, below their room, her dad stood beside a black Oldsmobile.

"I'll shoot her!" Ten yelled down at him. He heard rustling in the rooms around them, but no one came outside.

"What do you want?"

"A car. No one follows me."

"Done," Torry said. "Now give me my little girl."

Ten walked with Renda down the stairs. It wasn't easy. He almost tripped when she went off balance, but he managed to right both of them without falling. At street level, he walked slowly toward the Oldsmobile. "This the car?"

"Keys are in it," Torry said.

Ten walked closer to him, watched his face intently, waiting for him to make a move.

"My girl," Torry said. He looked worried. "Please, my little girl."

Ten saw where Torry's nose had bled. There were a few dark spots on his shirt from the blood as well. He lowered the pistol, and when Torry reached for his daughter, Ten stepped into him and brought the gun around and cracked him in the head. Torry fell like a lump.

"Daddy?" Renda tried to pull free.

Ten held tight to Renda. Torry had made a big mistake bringing his daughter. But maybe his work felt mundane to him; maybe he'd never had problems until now, Ten thought. "He would have killed me as soon as I let you go," he said into her ear.

"No, he wouldn't. He's an honest man."

"He's a killer," Ten said. "He killed my family."

"He holds to his word," she said. "He would have let you go. That was the bargain."

Ten opened the car door and shoved her into the car. When she was settled, he threw his backpack onto the center console and sat in the driver's seat. He started the car and drove out of the parking lot.

"You killed that man. You said you were after the source."

"He got in the way. Look, I didn't kill your dad. I could have. I could have killed you too." Ten's heart raced and his hands shook. His lips pulled together and he narrowed his eyes. "They would have killed me. Hell, they would have killed you if that was their job. Like your dad did to my family. Well, killing's not a job, it's a sickness."

"Then you've got it," she said.

"It makes me want to puke. I'm only doing what I have to do. They do it for money. They don't even know what I've done, if I've done anything wrong at all. They're hooked up with politicians and corporations. They could be after the wrong man." He clenched his teeth and shot her a dirty look. "They are after the wrong man."

"You'll never get away with this," she said.

"I don't want to," Ten said. "I just want to finish the job. They can kill me after that. I don't give a fuck."

Renda shook her head. "You don't mean that. She's dead, you're not."

Ten glared at her.

Renda held up her hands. "When my dad died, I didn't want to live either. Neither did my mom. She was lost. She drank. She treated me badly. She hated everyone and blamed everyone." She touched her cheek and went quiet. "Eventually, she snapped out of it."

"I don't want to snap out of it."

"I didn't either," Renda said quietly, "but I did. This isn't the best life, but it's a life. You'll find that's true for you too. I'm sure of it."

Ten shook his head. "I'm not so sure."

CHAPTER 4

"You're going south," Renda said. "Before you were going north. Do you think that'll slow my dad down?"

"That wasn't my thought at all. My thought was to lay low until the weekend."

Renda looked at her watch. "It is the weekend."

"One of the names on the list. I know him. He goes to the marina every weekend."

"You going to kill him on his boat?"

Ten shrugged.

"You could hardly stand shooting that other man. How are you going to do this in cold blood?"

"I'll close my eyes."

"This is not the life for you."

"Thanks for noticing, but it's the one I have now."

"But you'll just—" Ten's cell phone interrupted Renda. They both looked at his backpack. "Who could that be?" Renda asked.

Ten pushed his knee against the steering wheel and used both hands to open the backpack and pull out his phone. "Hello?"

"You don't know me," the voice said. "I'm Maria Tanner's friend."

"Is she okay?"

"I've got her hidden, but they're after me. I haven't heard from Russell and can't reach him."

"Russell's dead. Car bomb." Ten drove with one hand and held the phone to his ear with the other. "How do I know to believe you?"

"Maria said that you'd know by this: *the crosstalk on the switch has been fixed through a minor change in position.*"

"That was our last communication… before they packed up my stuff." Ten stared out the windshield, still not sure whether to believe the man on the phone or not.

"Are you still there?"

"Yes," Ten said. "You said she's alive."

"She's at a cabin outside of Detroit."

"Isn't that close to her offices? Shouldn't you get out of there?"

"Not for now. But we don't need you being followed here. When you're ready, pick up a new phone. You're using your work phone, right?"

"Are they tracking me?"

"I don't think so. This was a quick decision made by the wrong people. I have no idea what gave them such power, but they obviously don't know what to do with it. Beside the point," he said. "Just trash the phone for a new one. Call this number: 508-555-0999. Got that? Call that number and leave your new number. I'll get back with you."

"I want to hear her voice," Ten said. "The next time."

"I understand."

Ten hung up. He took a deep breath.

"What are you going to do?" Renda asked.

Ten pushed the window button and when it was down, he threw the phone out. "Yours is probably traceable." He shook his head. "It's okay. When I'm through, your dad should be close by. He can have you then." Ten hesitated. "You said he's an honest man?"

"Yes."

"He'll not shoot me as soon as you're free?"

"I don't know, now that you double-crossed him. But I don't think so."

Ten gave his attention back to driving. When he got to I-195, he headed toward Route 6 and the marina.

Renda removed her phone from her purse and pushed to dial.

"What are you doing?"

"Making sure he won't shoot you." She waited. "Daddy, I'm okay. He won't hurt me. You have to let him do what he needs to do." She waited while he spoke. "I know. I know. I'll tell him. Promise me." She listened some more. "I'll call you." She hung up.

"I don't believe this."

"You don't have to. He said there'll be others looking for you as long as they know you're alive. He said he's been reprimanded for failing to take you out. He's no longer under contract to kill you. You're the first job he's ever failed at, but he doesn't care what you're up to."

"He just wants you back. I know," Ten said.

"You have to protect me from whoever is after you." There was a waver in her voice. It seemed she believed her dad and was afraid of whoever else might be after Ten.

"They won't hurt you. They want me. As long as you don't know anything about my project."

"How can they be sure you didn't blab?"

"Psychological profile. I suspect they know me well enough that they know I won't put anyone else in jeopardy, especially a young girl."

"They do their homework."

"My project was secret. They have to do their homework."

"Why didn't they just kill you at work? A raid or something?"

"Too obvious. There are six of us on the project. Someone would put two and two together. Come to think of it, that's probably why I almost got hit coming out of the gym parking lot. And T-boned at an intersection."

Renda laughed like a high-school girl. "You're too quick for them. That's the trouble with tough guys, they're slow."

Ten had to laugh too, although nothing about what she said was funny. "Too confident," he said. "I suspect after a while their adrenaline doesn't peak, they don't get scared, so there's no extra oomph, as my mom used to say."

She turned her head to look out the window. "You are a scientist."

Ten passed a car at the side of the road and shook his head.

"What?" she prompted.

"I should have chucked my phone there. Maybe they'd think I'd stolen the car and stop to look for me. Now, if they know anything about Bower, they'll know where I'm heading."

"You know where he lives."

"Never had a reason to know."

"Then you don't have a choice. I guess you could always go after someone else on the list, someone who isn't close by, who isn't logical. You could always come back." Renda reached over and poked Ten's arm. "What do you think?"

"I think you're scared and are trying to figure out a way to stop me from including you."

She got serious. "You blame me?"

"I don't. But I'm going after Bower now, while I'm still alive. Even if I don't get any further than this, I'll have taken care of something."

"Not very optimistic."

"That comes after this is over." Ten watched the road signs and selected a turn-off where he saw signs for another cheap hotel. He'd ask for the ground floor this time. He pulled into the parking lot.

"Shouldn't we park somewhere else?"

"This is good." The two of them went inside and paid for the night. The room lay around the side of the main entrance, the lot a little darker, but it suited Ten. "This will do much better." Once inside, he dropped his backpack on the bed. "How's your honesty?"

"Like my dad's."

"Good. Promise me that you'll stay here while I shower."

"I promise. Where else would I go anyway?"

Ten reached out. "Your phone goes with me."

She huffed but gave it to him.

He planned to be fast, but he felt grimy. Even though he had to dress in the same clothes again, the shower felt refreshing. He was tired, but there wasn't time to sleep yet. He got out and toweled off, dressed, trying to rub a little smoothness back into his shirt to no avail. He brushed his hands through his hair. She was right. He didn't look very good with that color. He picked up her phone from the sink and walked into the main room.

The television was on very low and Renda lay with her feet toward the pillow and her elbows propping her up. "*Friends*," she said. "I've seen them all about a hundred times." She flicked the TV off.

"I need you to call your dad to come and pick up the car." He held out the phone.

"You want him to leave a new one?"

"Would he?"

She laughed and raised her eyebrows. "No," she said, shaking her head in disbelief.

"On second thought, dial him and hand me the phone."

Renda found the contact and poked it, then held the phone out to Ten. "All yours."

"Renda, dear, are you still okay?"

"I have her. She's fine."

"Let her go," Torry said.

"I will. Look I know you don't know what's going on much more than I do, but I'm just an engineer."

"Don't care. Not my business. Didn't she tell you, I'm not contracted anymore?"

"She did."

"Your wife loves you," Torry said then.

"What?"

"Your wife. She said to tell you she loved you before I killed you. That's all she seemed to care about. You should know."

Ten broke down and cried. He held the phone away from his face. He heard Torry talking, but didn't pull the phone any closer until he got his composure back. "Renda said that you're an honest man."

"This is true."

"I'm sure you know where we are. I want you to come and get your car. Get it out of here so no one else can track me. How long will that take?"

"Ten minutes." There was a slight pause. "You don't think you can outrun me, do you?"

Ten shook his head, but didn't answer Torry's question. "She's staying with me until I do what I have to do. You need to stay back. I don't care what you do after I finish business." He suspected Torry had no idea about the list, about Griffin Bower, or the project. He was a hired hand. And, for reasons Ten didn't even understand, he didn't blame Torry.

"Keep her safe, or I'll strip the skin off your body myself."

Ten looked over at Renda, saw how innocent she looked. No matter whose daughter she was, no matter what her father did for a living, she had her own demons to fight. "She'll be safe. I promise." He said it but didn't know if it was true. The one thing he did know was that Torry would always be close by. Torry would make sure she wasn't hurt. He clicked the phone off.

He pulled a few things from his backpack and threw her an apple and a power bar. They landed next to her on the bed. She rolled to her side. "What'd he say?"

"He's coming for the car. He wants me to keep you safe."

"Will you?" She picked up the apple and took a bite. "I'm pretty hungry."

"There's no room service in a place like this," Ten said.

"I'll bet there's takeout somewhere." She got up and walked over to the desk and opened the drawer. She produced a big fake smile and held up a local magazine. "Pizza good?"

"Sure. Why not."

In less than ten minutes, Ten peeked out the window and the car was gone. "Didn't even hear them take it away," he said.

"That's disheartening."

"Did you?"

"Yeah."

Ten cocked his head as he looked at her. "Really?"

"I did. So how you going to pay the pizza guy?"

Ten flipped open the hotel information pack that lay on the desk and slid an envelope out. He wrote *For the pizza guy* on the front of it, then stuffed thirty dollars inside. "That'll be plenty." He looked around and decided to use the Bible from the nightstand to hold the envelope down. At the door, he turned.

Renda held out her hand. "I'll do it." She went outside and placed the envelope on the sidewalk outside and put the Bible over it. It was right in front of their door.

"Thank you," Ten said when she stepped back inside.

"You're pretty smart."

It was easy to have the pizza kid put the pizza on the ground. He opened the envelope right away to be sure he wasn't stiffed, as Ten peered from the side of the window. He held the money up toward the door and yelled, "Thank you!" After he left, Renda retrieved the pizza and the Bible.

Chapter 5

Regardless how much he wanted to trust Renda, Ten still threw the bedspread and one of the pillows on the floor in front of the door to sleep on for the night. He figured she was as tired as he was and didn't expect an argument from her about whatever he chose. And he didn't get any complaint either. She removed her shoes and jacket and placed her purse on the nightstand. Then she went to the bathroom, came back, and climbed under the blanket fully clothed.

"Wake me if you hear anything outside," Ten said before turning off the light and nodding off.

When he woke, Renda was still fast asleep. He felt stiff and sore and stood slowly, rolling his shoulders and twisting his neck to get out the kinks. They had left a few pizza slices in the box, so he grabbed a cold slice and took a bite while standing over Renda. He couldn't help but wonder what it would be like to watch his own child sleep. He took a deep breath, felt the surge of emotion triggered by this thought. Tears almost come to his eyes, but receded. That wasn't his life any longer. He had a new life now. He had to take care of a little business, then help the other scientists stay alive. Maybe the only way to keep them alive was to kill everyone on Russell's list.

Russell. He thought about his friend and how he never knew what was really going on. Were they really friends? Or was Russell just not willing to kill innocent people no matter who they were? Ten would never know. He only knew that Russell had acted like his friend long enough to call him one.

Renda stirred and opened her eyes. She pulled the covers close to her chin. "How long have you been there? Staring at me?"

Ten held up most of the pizza slice. "Just woke up. Didn't mean to alarm you. Anyway, I was thinking, not staring."

"Well, it's creepy. Think with your eyes pointed somewhere else."

Ten turned back to his sleeping area and rolled up the bedspread, the pizza slice sticking out of his mouth, and threw it and the pillow in the corner near the nightstand. "You feel rested?"

Renda slid the covers down and sat on the side of the bed. Her tangled hair lay across her damp cheek. "Good enough."

"Today's the day," he said.

"You don't know he'll be there. Not for sure."

Ten grabbed a power bar from his backpack and held it toward her. "It's this or cold pizza."

"Cold pizza," she said.

"My kind of girl," Ten said automatically. Then he grinned.

"So?" she asked.

Ten handed her a pizza slice. "He'll be there. He always is. He talks about it all the time, brags how that even after his mother died, he spent the weekend on the water."

"Sounds like an asshole."

"Close enough." Ten didn't want to talk about him; he wanted to kill him. "How soon can you get ready?"

"Pretty quick." She reached for her purse and removed a hairbrush and threw it at him. "You first." She pointed at his head.

He looked in the mirror over the desk and had to laugh. "I look like a rooster."

Renda laughed too. "An ugly brown one."

Ten wandered into the bathroom and wet his hands, then ran them through his hair before using the brush. "All better."

"Close enough," she said when he came out. "Now it's my turn." She grabbed the brush as she passed him and went into the bathroom. She closed the door and he heard the toilet seat clank. In a minute, the toilet flushed and he heard water running.

He checked the gun. It had a magazine, which he figured out how to remove. He popped out the bullets and found that there were only four in there. He put them back and replaced the magazine. Four bullets, he thought. He rearranged his backpack so the knife handle was sticking out one of the side pockets, handy if he needed it. He grabbed the last slice of pizza and ate it, then ate the power bar. He still had a few more of them.

When Renda came out of the bathroom, she looked as though she'd gone to a spa. How did she do that? "You look refreshed. Did you shower and everything?"

"I know how to clean up."

"Yes, you do. You'll make some young man very happy one day."

She smiled at him, but the smile quickly fell into a grimace. She wrung her hands.

"What's bothering you?" Ten asked.

"You're going to protect me, right? From these other people after you? The government?"

"You'll be safe on two accounts. I know your dad's out there watching our every move. He won't even let them get close, I'm guessing. Or if he does, he'll be standing right next to them."

"You're using him to help you." It wasn't a question.

Ten smiled. "No, to protect you. I'm a dead man and I know it. It's just a matter of when."

Renda shook her head. "I don't believe that. You're a smart man, I can tell. And you're determined. You may not be a killer, but that won't stop you from doing what you need to do."

Ten picked up his backpack and pointed at her. "You are very optimistic. Let's hope you're right. You need anything more to eat?"

"I'm good."

"Then grab your jacket and purse and let's get out of here." He opened the door and reached for her hand. "We'll have to find a car to steal. Tricky at this time in the morning."

"It's five thirty, I doubt anyone's up but us."

"And your dad's people," Ten said.

Renda glanced into his eyes. She looked concerned. "Stay low." She took his hand and they were out the door, bent as low toward the ground as they could be.

Ten angled them into the corner of the parking lot as far away from the row of rooms as possible. He chose an older car, which would be easier to hotwire than some of the new ones. There was a pile of sweaters, jackets, gloves, and tools in the back seat, and he was sorry to have to steal it, but in the end, he had little choice. He had to steal a car, and this one was as good as any.

Renda climbed over into the passenger seat.

"You're getting good at that," Ten said.

"Shut up and drive."

He hotwired the car, got in, and backed out of the parking spot. Then he turned out of the lot and took the road he'd come in on the night before and headed toward I-195 South. They'd be there in no time.

"You don't think he'll get there early and head out already?"

"I hope not." Ten glanced into his rearview mirror. "Why does the mob always drive black cars?"

"They don't. Dad just likes them."

"Shit."

"Why, he can like whatever he wants."

"I didn't mean that. I think there's another car following us too. I don't recognize anyone inside—and it's not black." Ten swerved around an SUV and gunned the engine. The old car picked up pretty fast. He heard a few tools clank together in the back and something shift in the trunk.

"You can really pick a car," Renda said.

"Just stay low. I don't know what these people will do."

Renda slouched down in her seat. "You want your gun?"

"I don't know what good it will do. I never use a gun and couldn't hit anything if I wanted to. Besides, I only have four bullets left."

She shook her head. "I hope cold pizza wasn't my last meal."

"You're not funny."

"I know. I'm scared."

Ten passed a few more cars and noticed that Torry, or his people, fell back a little and the other car picked up. He needed it to be the opposite. Torry had to be between him and the other car for his plan of protection to work. Things weren't going well so far. He looked ahead and saw an exit. There was also a semi up ahead, so he passed the semi, switched to the far right lane, hoping he wasn't seen, and then slowed. Both of the other vehicles gained on him quickly. The moment his car passed the exit, Ten slammed on the brakes, threw the car into reverse, and backed over the safety zone far enough to take the exit. The other cars were too far gone and too far into traffic to follow him.

"We got about ten minutes," he said. He slammed through the stop sign at the end of the exit and turned toward the most populated area.

"Where are we going?"

"Same place. I want you to call your dad and tell him where we're headed. He has to get there first. Tell him we're being followed by what I suspect is the FBI or CIA or some such shit. Actually, when I think about it, it's probably that

International Security for Technological Innovation group. Yeah, that's who it must be." He shook his head. "No matter, just call him."

Renda dialed and got her dad right away. "Yeah, I'm okay, Daddy." After he said something else, she said, "We know. You have to get there first. He's going to let me go to you." She looked right at Ten.

He nodded. He'd let her go as soon as the job was done. "Tell him we're going to the Seaport Inn and Marina."

She told him and hung up. "He was hired by an outsider and didn't know the government was behind this. He doesn't want to get involved with any undercover government group. He said they don't play by the rules."

"Too late," Ten said.

Chapter 6

Ten knew the roads well enough to get him to where he wanted to be in record time. There were more people at the marina this early in the morning than he would have thought, but somehow it made sense. Anyone who wanted to spend the weekend on his boat would want to start early. He wondered how many slept on their boats overnight. Boats. He had to laugh at himself for thinking of them as boats. It was a yacht club after all, not a boat club.

He pulled in and looked over at Renda. "I'm sorry, but you've got to go with me. Don't worry."

She pointed toward his shaking hand. "You're worried."

"I'm scared. I don't know how to do this. I don't know if I can. And I don't know what's going to happen afterward. This could easily be my last day alive."

She stared at him. A tear accumulated at the corner of her eye. "Don't say that." She turned away. "I don't want to see that."

Ten reached over and grabbed her hand and squeezed it. "You'll be okay. I promise you with everything I have." He took a deep breath and opened his door.

Renda crawled over the center console and out his door and stood next to him. She looked over his shoulder and then around the area.

"They're not here yet. Maybe we have time," Ten said.

"Time for what?"

"To take care of this before any of them arrive. Before this gets really complicated." Ten walked at a good pace toward the docks, holding Renda's wrist.

She jerked her hand away and rubbed her wrist. "You don't have to hold me so tight. I'll go with you."

It was too late now to make any other plans, to fall back, to hide, to run, so Ten let her walk with him. This was it for him anyway. She could stay or go. An attendant stood at a small covered shack, and was kind enough to instruct Ten toward Griffin Bower's yacht. Once on the boardwalk, Ten chose not to turn around to see who was behind him, or if anyone were behind him, yet he noticed Renda continually glanced around even though she stuck close beside him.

With each step toward Bower's boat, Ten let in a more of the memories from the past two days little by little. First, he relived Groucho's death and the blazing fire, then Russell's car exploding, then Amy lying on the bed with the pillow over her head. There was the torture of having to kill the man at the hotel too. His first kill. And the fear he felt while negotiating with Torry. With each memory, heartache, pain, and anger grew into hatred fueled by adrenaline. As he got closer to Bower's yacht, his hands quaked at his sides. Ten spied Bower's yacht ahead of them and leaned into his walk as though about to run, but he kept his pace, purposeful, powerful, targeted.

When they arrived, Ten helped Renda onto the boat first. Then he stepped up. He heard voices on the other side of cockpit and walked around toward the more open front of the boat. Griffin stood talking with another man, reprimanding him for something, and saw Ten as he came around. He stopped talking and his eyes went wide. The other man swung around, a young man in his mid-twenties. He looked upset.

"You can go," Ten said. "We have business."

"No, stick around, Carl," Griffin said.

But the kid looked as though he knew what Ten was up to, and was glad to be excused by anyone. He rushed around Ten and Renda and off the boat.

Griffin still hadn't said anything.

Ten took a few more steps toward him, then swung at him, hit his jaw, and Griffin fell to the floor.

"What the hell?" His face grew angry, his eyes narrowed. "You're supposed to be dead."

"Amy's dead," Ten said. He took another step toward Griffin. His heart raced, his lip quivered. His hatred built.

"You won't get away with this. This project's too important. You could ruin everything."

"Oh, I plan to," Ten said.

Griffin got up slowly. In a cocky voice he said, "You won't get the chance, buddy." He pointed at Renda. "And your little chicky here won't either. You're dead, you know that," he said to her. He looked Ten in the eyes. "Anyone who gets near you is as good as dead."

Ten hit him again, this time in the stomach.

Griffin crumbled to the ground. He laughed. "You won't get out of here alive."

Ten brought his backpack around, removed the gun, and pointed it at Griffin. His hands shook uncontrollably. He feared he wouldn't even hit Griffin if he pulled the trigger.

Ten heard Renda screech and saw her step back, placing her hands over her face, but not her eyes. He turned slightly toward her. "Don't watch this."

"Don't do it," she said. "Please."

Griffin, his hands close to his face, pursed his lips. "I didn't kill anyone. You know that, don't you? I'm an operative, part of a greater project, just like you." Griffin changed his position on the matter once the gun was on him. "Seriously. I can probably get you off the hook. Decisions can change. I know—"

"The other decision makers." Ten didn't believe him. "I know who they are too."

"You can't."

"Enough talk." Ten extended his arm and put three out of the four bullets into Griffin's chest. It didn't make him feel any better. His arm dropped to his side. It didn't stop him from thinking of Amy. It didn't wipe any of the images from his mind. It only added another one: Griffin Bower slumped to the floor of his yacht, bleeding from the chest. Dead. Griffin's death didn't get Ten off the hook from anything and he knew it.

But it was done.

He turned around and saw that Renda was curled on the floor of the yacht.

"You killed him," was all she said.

He walked past Renda and jumped onto the boardwalk. There could have been police or security running his way, but there weren't. No one stood on the walkway. But at the end of it stood Torry. As Ten approached, Torry pulled out a pistol and pointed it at him. Ten didn't stop walking. "She's alive," Ten said. "You can go get her."

Torry held the gun all the while Ten approached. He lowered it when Ten got within five feet of him. "You kept her safe?"

"The best I knew how," Ten answered. He wanted to hate Torry for what he'd done, but knew how it all worked. The low man on the totem pole gets the dirty work, the blame, the punishment, and the people at the top get off scot-free. Well, not this time. Not this time.

Torry shrugged. "I kept you safe. For now. I'd be careful if I were you."

"I will." Ten turned and saw that Renda had gotten over her initial shock and was jogging down the boardwalk in his direction. "She's a good kid."

Torry let Ten walk past and asked, "What was that?" He obviously knew little about what was going on. For as much as he might think he's a big shot, he's just another chump, another pawn.

"That's one," Ten said over his shoulder.

Torry bent down to raise Renda into his arms.

On the way toward the stolen car, Ten passed two men who looked as though they'd been knocked out. Another two men, obviously with Torry for the way they dressed, stood with their arms crossed, watching Ten meander toward his ride.

Next thing he needed was a phone. There were scientists to save.

Second Kill

CHAPTER 7

After swapping stolen cars twice, Ten drove the last leg toward Detroit. He had been out of touch for so long that he almost felt safe. He knew he wasn't. The air drifting into the window of the old Saab felt fresh, even more so after a soft morning shower that had recently stopped. Earlier, he pulled from I-90 into a mall well past Buffalo, NY, in hope of picking up a cheap cell phone from Walmart. He parked in a far corner of the lot where he left the vehicle to be found by police. His first stop was an ATM where he removed another five hundred dollars. His account was still open, which made him feel lucky. His backpack swelled with high-protein food, several bottles of water, two rolls of toilet paper, the knife he'd taken from home, and the gun with one bullet left in it. That might be his next project: see about getting more bullets. He figured Torry's gun wouldn't be traceable. At least he hoped so.

Ten had slept for a few hours at a rest stop along I-90 before getting on I-75 toward Detroit. He felt refreshed. The morning rain had helped him wake up, too. He could hardly believe the events of the past few days, and tried to keep them from entering his mind. He wanted plans, not memories of his murdered wife and friend, at the moment. He considered two avenues: going after the people on the DECISION MAKERS list or on the TEAM list. He decided to take it in stride, whoever was closest. If each scientist had a bodyguard as Russell said, then there wasn't much more that he could do… maybe. At the moment, he knew Maria Tanner was alive. Well, not really. What he knew about her came from the person who claimed to be her bodyguard. Ten had yet to talk with Maria directly. He needed to call the number he was given. That's why it was important to him to get a new phone.

He moved easily into the store and walked deep into it, near the rear where the electronics were located. He found the phone display and sidled up to the glass case to check them out.

A young clerk came over right away. "Looking for a phone?"

"Yes, I figured it was about time."

The kid, who had a shaggy head of blond hair and thick glasses, made a funny face. "Really?"

"Really," Ten said. "The rest of my family has them, I figured it was my turn."

"Well, you came to the right place. We have the best plans and pretty much any phone you would like." He bent over and pulled an Android from inside the counter. "This is a popular phone and it's fairly easy to use." He handed it to Ten and leaned in to show him a few key points about the phone.

Ten listened for a few minutes and asked about the price, then agreed it would work. The kid proceeded to fill out the paperwork and set up the phone. He asked for a name and address, but never asked to see Ten's ID, which was good, since Ten gave him false information all the way through. For additional contact, Ten used Russell's cell number, then said, "We just moved from Massachusetts."

"No problem."

The transaction took about an hour. The kid handed Ten the rebate information and his paperwork. Before leaving, Ten asked about a sporting goods store where he might buy a hunting license, and the kid gave him directions. Once outside he called the number Maria's bodyguard had given him. He left his name and new number. Short and sweet.

In the lot, Ten found an old Toyota Tercel, light blue, jacked it, and headed for the sporting goods store to buy bullets.

Glen's Adventures sat between a tobacco shop and a hair salon. It took up over half the space of the tiny strip mall. The shabby signs looked as though they'd been there for decades without maintenance. Ten pulled up and parked far to one side of the lot and walked to the store. He went inside, pulled his pistol out of his backpack, and asked the older gentleman with a balding head and intense eyes if he had bullets for it.

"How many rounds you want?"

"It's my dad's old gun and I don't know anything about it."

The man dropped the magazine into his hand and looked at Ten. "First off, it's illegal to be carrying a concealed weapon, and loaded too. You might want to get a permit for this thing if you're going to haul it around like this."

"Should I do that in my own state?"

The man gave Ten a quizzical look and cocked his head.

"My dad's from here, but I'm living in Massachusetts. Shouldn't I get the permit there?"

"If you're going to transport it, keep it in your trunk. Unloaded."

Ten smiled at the man. "Will do. So what kind of gun is it?"

Again, the man gave Ten a sideways glance. "Your dad didn't tell you?" He didn't wait for an answer. "Glock 19. You want a box of rounds." He placed the gun on the counter. "Let's call them rounds instead of bullets, shall we?"

"Make that two boxes. And another clip," Ten said.

The man turned around to a shelf filled with boxes of rounds. "It's called a magazine," the man said over his shoulder.

"How many rounds does a magazine hold?"

"Fifteen." The man slapped two boxes of rounds onto the counter. "One in the chamber makes sixteen." He picked up the pistol and removed the round from the chamber and the one from the magazine. He slapped them both onto the counter next to the boxes. "Here's the two you had in there."

"Only one in the magazine." Ten was starting to get the point.

The man nodded. He had a little smirk on his face.

"I might as well learn how to shoot the thing."

The man walked to another area of the counter and brought out a second magazine. "You're lucky I have one."

"I am lucky." While Ten waited for the total, his phone rang. He held up his hand. "I have to get this." He swung around and walked away from the counter.

"It's Maria. I'm okay. Ben is taking good care of me. Here he is." She handed the phone off.

"Where are you?" Ben asked. Ten told him approximately where he was on I-75. "Directions."

"Hold on." Ten spun back around. "Pen and paper?"

The man behind the counter slid a pen and paper to Ten. "Shoot." He realized what he'd said and looked up at the clerk, smiled, and shrugged. He wrote down the directions. "I suspect it'll be an hour or so before I get there?"

The man at the other end hung up.

Ten paid for his purchases and left the store. When he got to the car, he loaded both magazines, and loaded the chamber. Sixteen rounds in the Glock and fifteen in the second magazine. He laid both on the seat beside him. He drove for a half hour or so. By the time he pulled off the highway near Newport, Ten felt a little groggy. He drank a whole bottle of water and ate two power bars hoping to get his system rolling again. It seemed to work.

He followed Ben's directions to a wooded area and pulled off onto a dirt road to drive farther back into the woods. He didn't like how little he could see around him.

Sure enough, though, there was a small cabin tucked away in a clearing just as he was told.

With his heart in his throat, Ten grabbed his backpack, threw the spare magazine in an outside pocket, half zipped it, and grabbed the Glock from the seat beside him. He glanced around the area. No movement and no sign of anyone being around except for an old pickup parked to the side of the cabin. He opened the door, got out, and that's when bullets started flying.

Chapter 8

The shots came from the driver's side of the car. Ten rolled to the front of the car and scurried to the other side where he hunkered close to the ground next to the Tercel's passenger door. There had only been three shots. They came close, but didn't hit him, so he suspected they were either shooting pistols, which are harder to aim, or they didn't want to kill him. The latter didn't make sense, since he was supposed to be dead already. A rifle would have had more range and a scope would have corrected for accuracy problems. He had no idea where this information came from, but suspected years of watching television and movies, and reading must have offered up some answers just when he needed them.

None of that helped though. He felt trapped. And he knew he wouldn't be able to hit anything if he shot back. First, he'd have the same aiming problem they did, and second, he hadn't even seen them.

He closed his eyes and took a deep breath. When he opened his eyes, he noticed a tallish man in a gray suit, the tie removed and the shirt collar open, slip around the side of the cabin near the pickup. The man put a finger to his lips, as though Ten was about to shout something to him. He held a gun. With his other hand, he, most likely Ben, held up one finger, then two, then three. After that, he put his hand in his pocket and pulled out what looked like an aerosol bottle with a hand grenade pin and ring hanging from it. Ben lowered his head toward Ten and Ten nodded, letting him know that he knew the drill. Ben nodded. On the third nod, he came around to the side of the cabin and threw the grenade between Ten and the people who had shot at him. It went off with a billow of smoke and Ten ran for Ben, while a few rounds went off.

Ten dived near the truck.

"You're okay," Ben said, not asking. "Now stay here while I take care of them." Ben disappeared behind the cabin. Smoke continued to blur the Tercel and most of that side of the cabin. Ten held his Glock, never having taken one shot. The safety was still on. He leaned against the truck door, noticed how much more room there was under the truck and felt lucky for the third time that day for always stealing low-riding vehicles, which made it more difficult for anyone to shoot under.

It wasn't long before Ten heard two shots. He waited, heard footsteps, held his gun out as though he were going to shoot it, and then Ben rounded the corner through the smoke, his pistol in his hand, hanging at his side. "Done, but we're hardly safe here." He banged on the side of the cabin and yelled, "Let's go!" He helped Ten to stand up. "High-intensity smoke grenade," he said, explaining what he'd thrown.

Maria looked very frazzled when she came around the back of the cabin. Her curly hair always looked a bit messed anyway, but now it looked as though she had just woken from a long nap. She was in her forties, with a slight build, her eyes wide set. She carried what looked like a very heavy bag. She ran over to Ben, dropped the bag on the ground, and wrapped her arms around him.

"In the truck," he told her. He picked up the bag and handed it to Ten, who already had his backpack slung across his shoulder. "It's heavy. Munitions." He was a man of few words.

She got into the passenger side and scooted near the center. Ben drove. Ten sat next to Maria with the munitions bag crammed between them on the floor, and his backpack sitting on top of it. "So what's going on?" he asked as soon as he shut the door.

"You two probably know more about that than I do," Ben said as he backed around and headed for the main road.

"Maybe I can guess," Ten said.

Maria turned to him. "I'm glad I'm not the only one alive." She looked like she was in shock.

"Me too," Ten said. "I thought I was working on nanobots that could be used in surgery for vascular repair, heart problems, that sort of thing, but once I saw the list of team players—"

Maria interrupted. "What list?"

"Russell gave me a list."

"Good old Russell," Ben said without looking over.

"You knew him?" Ten asked.

"Trained with him. Several of us on this mission trained together." Ben shook his head. "That was their mistake."

"Why?"

"Because we were still friends. We talked." He glanced around Maria, who sat quietly between them, and said, "I'm sorry about Russell."

"Me too," Ten said again. It seemed appropriate.

"So?" Ben asked.

"Maria?" Ten took her hand.

"I'm okay. We just didn't sleep much last night. With all this going on…"

"I understand. So," he patted her hand, "you know too, don't you?"

She shrugged. "I thought we might be working toward some kind of all-encompassing disease control." She started to tear up. "You know there's a lot of progress in that area."

Ten finished for her. He aimed his explanation toward Ben. "If we can adjust a DNA strand to eliminate the propensity for a certain disease, then we can also use a nanoswitch—like the ones I've been working on for the past seven years—to *create* disease as well. To kill."

"But you have to get your switches into the body, right?" Ben wasn't seeing the big picture yet.

Ten said, "What if the government put the switches inside… say, a vaccination? One that every child has to have when they're young?" Ten stopped for only a moment, to let the idea settle. "What if one of us were working on a control system where we could interface with each switch separately. After all, every one of my switches has a code, sort of like a frequency, that it responds to. Let's say we can reach these switches, punch in the codes, via cell phone towers?"

"Everyone would be susceptible to the disease," Ben said.

"The government could start with one or two deaths from one 'area code,' so to speak. Then grow it out as slowly or quickly as they'd like."

"But why kill people? Population control?"

"Or political? Or economic?" Ten said. "If there were a plague of some kind, our unemployment numbers would change dramatically. More people would have jobs all of a sudden. Which would help our economic situation as well. Maybe not fix it, but it could make a difference."

"It's not just the government, is it?"

Shocking both of them, Maria burst out with, "Hackers could kill off millions of people. Or another country could buy the technology from…" she looked from Ben to Ten and back, then blurted, "one of us."

"But we can't put the whole thing together," Ten said.

"We know enough to help another country do that though. Each of us has access to a huge part of the project," she said.

"A sixth. There are six team members." Ben paused, then said to Ten, "I take it that Russell gave you the list."

"Before they killed him."

Ben shook his head. "Wow, that man was good. I can't imagine how he got that much information from the inside." Ben pulled off the highway onto a side road. The car swerved around a curve, then straightened out.

Ten noticed that they were going south. "Washington, DC?"

Ben nodded. "Not going to be easy to get there."

"The truck?" Ten asked.

"They know where we were, they probably know where we're going. The truck, a stolen car, ATMs, you name it, they'll track us."

"That's why they haven't closed my account," Ten said with some recognition.

Maria lowered her chin. "We're not safe anywhere."

Ben put his arm around her. "If I would have known, I'd never…"

Ten knew what he alluded to. They were lovers, and if Ben never told Maria any more than Russell told him, then this whole situation must have turned into a shocking discovery for her. Ten was surprised Maria stuck around after that, that she didn't panic and try to get away. But then where would she go? Ten slouched in his seat and peered into the rearview mirror. "Hey, isn't that—"

Ben tapped Ten's arm and shook his head.

Ten shut up.

Ben obviously knew they were being followed, but Maria didn't. And she never asked what Ten was about to say either.

Before long, Ben took a sharp, right-angle turn onto a back road. The car behind them swung into action too. "In the bag, you'll find another smoke grenade. The high intensity ones are marked."

"What will that do?"

"Give us time to get out of the truck and hide. We don't need them to call reinforcements." Ben brought his arm back around and patted Maria's leg. "You can do this."

"I trust you," she said, but she sounded rather weak in her response.

"Say when." Ten pulled the grenade from the bag and zipped it back up. He held the grenade up and put his finger through the steel ring connected to the pin. He rolled down the window and leaned out.

"Be careful!" Ben yelled.

Ten pulled the safety ring and threw the grenade. Even before it went off, Ben slammed on the brakes and turned off the road. Smoke filled the air behind them. Everyone jumped out. Maria followed Ben. He held her hand and pulled her into a gulley from what Ten could see. Ten, on the other hand, held tightly to the munitions bag in one hand and his backpack in the other as he ran in the opposite direction into the woods. He parked himself behind a tree. He barely heard gunshots, but when he looked back at the truck, the windows were out. Several more shots rang out, but not toward him, toward Ben and Maria. Whoever followed them may not have known Ten was with them, or who he was. They may have been waiting for Maria and Ben to leave the cabin, which meant they were out to kill Maria. "Bastards," Ten said. He removed his Glock, shouldered his backpack, grabbed the munitions bag, and ran in the direction of where the bullets were coming from. They were probably in the woods, trying to avoid the smoke and get closer to Ben and Maria. Ten figured he'd come up from behind.

On the other side of the smoke screen, he noticed no one was in the car that had followed them, but it was still idling. He pushed farther back into the woods and made a wider swath as he walked. No one had stayed with the car. He knew where the others were going and wondered what more he could do besides come up on them from the rear. He set his gun down and unzipped the bag. This time he rummaged through it. All sorts of weapons he didn't recognize nor knew how to use were inside. The machine gun actually scared him. Without practice, he knew he could do more harm than good. He zipped the bag back up.

He backtracked enough to put two bullets into the gas tank of the truck. Then he ran to the other car, something mid-sized he didn't recognize and didn't take the time to search for its name. He threw the munitions bag into the back seat, jumped into the driver's seat and drove through the smoke in the direction of the truck, hoping he was accurate enough to pull to the right of the truck without hitting it. He was.

He got out with his Glock held in both hands and raised up like some television cop waiting to raid a house. He had no idea what he was doing.

When he heard the first shots, his heart sank, but he looked around the side of the truck anyway. He couldn't see anything until one of the men rushed from behind one tree toward another one, closer to where Ten last saw Ben and Maria. His hands sweated. He closed his eyes, then he ran toward the woods, lifted the pistol, and shot four times at the tree where the man hid. It was enough surprise to get both men to turn toward Ten with their guns. In an instant, one of the men dropped his pistol and yelled. The other one hid again. And Ten dropped to the ground and scurried over to the ditch along the road. Luckily, it was dry.

Ben appeared to automatically know what Ten was thinking when he ambushed the men. So Ten went with that assumption. He turned and crawled back toward where the car had originally been. When he glanced up, he saw one of the men had fallen back, probably the injured one. Well, he'd soon find the car missing. Ten pushed on. He heard another shot behind him and raised his head to look back. Another shot rang out and Ten felt his shirt scuff and then felt a burning sensation in his arm.

He was hit.

CHAPTER 9

He lowered his head into the ditch and waited. They'd be coming after him, now that they knew he had a gun. He rolled onto his back. Pain shot through his arm when he moved, but it wasn't as bad as he'd always thought it might be if he got shot. Why anyone would think of such things is irrelevant. He had thought about them. Lucky for him, his left arm had been hit and he was right-handed. He let his head relax against the ground only for a minute. When he heard someone running through the woods, he raised up from the waist, pointed, and let three rounds fly. The man dropped. Without thinking, Ten jumped up.

"Hold up." When Ten turned around, the other man stood near him with his pistol pointed at Ten's chest. The man's hand was bloody. "I should shoot your ass right now."

"I wouldn't," came Ben's voice from the side.

When the man turned his head, Ben kicked and the gun went flying. Ten delivered two body punches and the man dropped to his knees. He looked over at Ben. "You won't get away. You know ISTI."

"You can kill innocent scientists? The same ones who performed their duties honorably for our country?" Ben didn't wait for an answer. "You don't get it, do you?" Ben walked over and pushed the man to the ground. "Hands on the back of your head."

The man complied. "They know too much."

"They've done nothing."

"But they could." Blood ran down the man's hand and sleeve of his jacket.

Maria walked up behind Ben. She wore a fashionable pantsuit. She pulled her blouse from the pants and used her teeth to tear a strip from it. She then walked over and wrapped the man's hand. "Keep it compressed." She pulled his injured hand near the other one and let him clasp them together, still over his head.

"You see?" Ben said. "They've done nothing. Since when did we, or any government agency, punish someone because they *could* do something?"

"This must be more important. Too risky."

Ben shook his head. "Should we feel the same about you?"

The man didn't respond.

Ben patted the man down, found a cell phone, and crushed it under his heel. "I'll check the other guy." He walked away. No one ever said what to do, so Ten held his gun on the man while they waited.

Maria stepped closer to Ten. "I'm sorry I've been so out of it. Really, I'm just exhausted." She looked at his wound. "Mostly tore your skin. Probably hurts though."

"Good to hear," Ten said. "There's some water in my backpack. It's in the car. I parked it near the truck."

"I saw that. Good idea in case we had the chance to run for it."

"He's alive!" Ben yelled from inside the woods.

Ten waved the barrel of his pistol. "You can go to your friend. He'll need your help."

The man cocked his head enough to glance at Ten quizzically, then lowered his hands and stood. He held his hands in front of him, keeping pressure on the wound.

"So, you and Ben?" Ten asked Maria.

"For two years. I never knew…" She stared off into the woods. "I was so pissed that he didn't tell me, that he just let me believe everything was normal."

Ten put his arm around her. "I know. But there was no way he could have done that. For sure then, your life would have been in danger. He probably thought it would all be fine once we made our discoveries. How could he know this would happen? You probably had to keep information from him too. This was a secret project."

"Logical," she said. "But it really hurt my feelings."

"They killed my wife," Ten said. He didn't know if he was trying to put things into perspective for her, trying to put them into perspective for himself, or if he just needed to tell someone, to say it, to let it out of him. A small rush of emotion flowed through him after he said it.

"I'm so sorry." She hugged him. "And your friend too."

"My bodyguard… and friend," Ten agreed.

Ben waited a few feet away. "We have to go. I think he'll be okay back there, but they'll have to tell ISTI where we were headed."

"You think these two will be okay? They won't be killed for failing?" Ten asked.

"The agency has enough trouble on their hands." Ben led everyone to the car. When they all got settled, he backed around and drove out of the woods. Back on the road, he said, "We'll head west, dump this monster of a car, and find another one as soon as we can. Then we'll head to Cleveland."

"What's in Cleveland?" Ten asked. He reached into his backpack, refilled the magazine for his Glock, then snapped it into place.

"Long-term parking." Ben winked.

"How far is it?"

"Three and a half, four hours. Maybe a bit longer. I'll take back roads. By the way, you did good back there," Ben said.

"Who knew?" Ten set his gun on top of his pack.

"Russell told me you were quick. That you were studying martial arts at the gym. He used to joke that once you were done with your project, he wanted to recruit you." Ben smiled. He had a kind smile, honest. Ten could see how Maria could fall for him. He was a nice man.

Not far up the road, they jacked another car, an old Honda, with several rust patches. They headed west on 24. "We'll turn around after we jack another car. If they're watching closely, they'll think we're going west." He glanced around Maria. "Your list. There must be someone west of here."

Ten pulled the plastic bag from his shirt pocket and opened it. He said, "Crocket Point's in Oregon, isn't it?"

"Yes." Maria reached for the paper and took it from Ten. "Let me see that." She perused the lists. "Practical Robotics is in Seattle, and Smithers Pharmaceuticals is in California, outside San Francisco. Where's ISTI?"

"New York, believe it or not," Ben said.

"Then that's three out west, and the rest on the eastern seaboard." Maria handed the paper back, reached out, and turned on the radio, then adjusted the dial until she found what sounded like news radio. "I doubt we'll hear much, but it would be good to know if any of the others made it."

"We wouldn't know anyway," Ten said. "The news claimed I was killed in the fire that burned my house down." He thumped his chest. "And I'm still here. I suspect they'll fake the news so we don't know what's going on."

She flicked it off. "No use, then."

Ben turned it back on with the volume low. "Never hurts to be aware." Ben settled in his seat. "Besides, I wonder if anyone knows about that list of yours? If they don't know you have it, then why would they try to fool you? People die every day."

"Don't know the answer to that one, I'm afraid. I just know they faked my death." Ten looked out the window as they passed houses along the highway. He rubbed his arm. "Stopped bleeding, but it still hurts."

Maria turned and spread the gap in his shirt. "Looks okay. We'll keep an eye on it."

Several hours later, Ben followed signs for long-term parking at the Cleveland Hopkins airport. He pulled off the road and they got out. He held out his hand. "Cell phones?" One by one, he crushed their phones under his heel. "We'll walk the rest of the way."

They came to the Orange Lot and walked past the attendant. Ben waved and the attendant waved back. "The longest line of cars," he said. Ten and Maria followed. "Look for the dates on the tickets on the dash. We're looking for early today or yesterday." It didn't take long and Ten spotted a Ford Focus, dark green, with a ticket dated the day before. Ben opened the munitions bag and pulled out a thin metal strap, shoved it next to the window jam, jerked it slightly, and pulled up. The car door lock snapped and Ben opened the door. "Let's go." Before long, they were out of the lot and driving southeast toward DC—all back roads.

CHAPTER 10

"Sharon Pontrelli first," Ten said as they entered the outskirts of Washington, DC. "We try to save the innocent people before we go after the decision makers."

"Crowell-Picker Labs is north of the city," Maria said.

"We know she won't be there." Ten narrowed his eyes. "We may be able to talk with someone close to her. That might help. It'll be tricky. I'd like to come up with a plan."

"I've talked with Sharon a few times," Maria said.

"More of us were in touch with one another than they might have thought." They had taken turns driving and everyone had gotten a chance to sleep a few hours. Ten felt good behind the wheel, like he was getting somewhere.

"Did you talk with her too?" Maria asked.

"No."

"Then who'd you talk with?"

"Just you, and Roger at Practical Robotics."

"Makes sense. You're both involved with nanos, right?"

"Roger is a genius. He's perfected multi-purpose nanobots that can disassemble and reassemble for different functions. Typically, there are different nanobots designed for each different type of job, so being able to refocus a bot that's already in your system is a big deal. He uses some kind of combination of gyros and magnetics. We never got that far into it. Our calls were always monitored. All I did was work on switching and coding technologies—part hardware, part software."

Maria laughed. "Yeah, he's the genius. All you did was work on the heart of the system as far as control is concerned."

"Yeah." He pulled into the parking lot of a restaurant called Cassios. "We stop to eat?" It wasn't really a question. "We can talk over how we might find out about Sharon."

Ben, who had been staring out the window while Ten and Maria talked, nodded. "Probably should. Don't know where we'll have to look for your friend."

"Or anyone else," Ten said as they all got out of the car.

Ben leaned over the roof of the car to look at Ten. "We'll have to be fast. We're in their backyard. You never know who's been called in."

"I trust you'll know when it's not safe," Maria said while reaching out to him.

They held hands going into the restaurant. Ben sat facing the door, Maria beside him. Ten wasn't comfortable with his back to the door, but at the same time he knew Ben was alert, and more knowledgeable about these things. After ordering, Ben got a little fidgety. Their food hadn't shown up yet.

"What's going on?" Ten asked. Maria didn't appear to notice anything wrong.

"Too many men with suits at this time of day. I don't like it."

The waiter brought their food and sat it down. Ben leaned around him so he always had his eye on the room. Ten got nervous about Ben's nervousness, but he didn't turn around.

Maria looked up at the waiter and thanked him. Ten and Ben followed suit, but without looking him in the eye.

"Eat fast," Ben said.

"Not the best thing to say," Ten said. "Maybe we should get it to go."

"Maybe." Ben slid out of his seat. "Let's go."

"We haven't paid," Maria said.

"Or eaten," Ten said.

Ben opened his wallet and threw down a fifty. "No time. You two go out the back. I'll head them off and be right with you."

Ten still had the car keys. He took Maria's hand and walked toward the kitchen. They pushed through a swinging door. The waiter started to walk up to them. He opened his mouth to protest and Ten shook his head and held up his hand. The waiter wasn't the confrontational type, thank goodness. He stepped aside and Ten pulled Maria behind him. Out the back, they ran around the building. No one appeared to be waiting outside, which seemed stupid. But then, arrogance can make smart people dumb sometimes. Ten unlocked the passenger side of the car. He heard a shot from inside the restaurant and ran for the door. Inside, one man lay on the floor, while the other one had a gun on Ben.

Ten didn't wait for an invitation; he dove, arms spread, into the back of the knees of the man holding the gun. The gun went off, but Ben remained standing. Ten lay on the floor with the man on top of him. Ben kicked the man in the jaw and he flopped over. Ten crawled from under him and stood.

"Nice move." Ben slapped Ten's back.

The two of them burst through the door. Ten jumped in and started the car. By the time Ben hit the seat, Ten was already backing out of the parking spot.

"You didn't kill them?" Maria asked quietly. Her hand rested on his thigh.

"No." He hesitated a moment, then said, "But I wouldn't let them kill me either."

Ten pulled out of the lot and turned right, the easiest turn to make. He drove straight until Ben told him to take a left, then a mile or so later, he was instructed to again take a left.

"They probably know where we're going," Ten said.

"They'd be wrong," Ben said.

"Aren't we going to Crowell-Picker?"

"She's dead," Ben said

Maria's hands went to her face. "No. How could you know that?"

"Back there. The man I shot was her bodyguard. He didn't kill her, the man with him did." He nodded toward Ten. "The man you knocked down. Her bodyguard couldn't do it." He took a deep breath. "Most of us are honest men. We'll kill to protect our people and our government, but we're not trained to…" He never finished that sentence. For Ten he didn't have to. Russell had already told him.

Ten let up on the gas when he saw he was speeding. They didn't need to get stopped with a stolen car. "Sounds like whoever made this decision also started a complete breakdown of his own system."

"Worse than that," Ben said.

"What do you mean?"

Ben cleared his throat. "Some of the operatives have been murdered too. The whole ISTI group appears to be going through a complete turnover." He shook his head. "It's hard to know who to trust inside or out."

"They would have come after you eventually anyway," Ten suggested.

"Pretty much what they're doing now."

"Where are we going?" Ten asked.

"A hotel. It's where the secretary of Technological Innovations is staying at the moment. He's in town."

"Eric Webber? He's on the list," Maria noted.

Ben didn't answer.

Maria didn't seem to be able to stand it though. She said, "You're going to kill him."

"And then Jacob Metzger." Ben didn't appear to be upset about it, only determined. "He's the mission chief. He's half the problem. With him gone, the group has some serious internal problems."

"Won't that just make things worse?" Ten asked.

"Absolutely. Blow ISTI apart from the inside."

"Won't they scatter?"

"I don't think they'll stop looking for us, if that's what you mean," Ben said. "But eventually, we're going to get Jasper Ignato. He's the head man. This had to have been ordered by him."

"All for the sake of saving this technology for, for…" Ten didn't know where to go with his sentence.

"Maybe not keep it safe, but to sell it to the highest bidder," Ben said.

"Don't tell me there's a timeline on this. Don't tell me you think it's already been sold and it just has to be delivered." Ten's hands suddenly got sweaty. "This isn't good."

"Let's focus," Maria said, interrupting the theorizing. "One person at a time. Who is it?"

"Eric Webber," Ben said with assurance. "Because I know where to find him." In a few more minutes, Ben directed, "Take this exit."

"Heart of the city," Ten said.

"Downtown," Ben confirmed.

Maria said, "We don't have a choice, do we? We have to keep going."

"Trust me, babe. But, you're right; we have no choice," Ben said.

They drove into the heart of Washington, DC, to Independence Avenue. "Pull over here," Ben said. "We'll walk. We're going to the Hyatt. He holds a suite there. But first, we'll get cleaned up, get some new clothes, and get back on the street."

"It's the middle of the day; don't you think they'll know where we are?"

"Things are breaking up already. They're confused. Trust me on this. We're good." Ben never seemed in doubt.

Ten worried anyway. At the moment, he wondered what he had actually thought he might be able to do on his own. He shot Griffin Bower, but that was nothing like this, nothing like going after ISTI itself, or attempting to get to a government official.

Ben checked them in at a b&b on a back street. He knew the woman who owned it. "May, how are you?" They bantered for a few minutes. Ben introduced Maria and Ten using different names, which Ten hardly heard. He just waved when pointed at.

"What happened?" May asked about Ten's flesh wound.

Ben laughed. "An accident. You don't want to know."

"Well, if you need anything…" She handed over the keys.

Ten and Maria followed Ben upstairs. He dropped his munitions bag on the floor. "You two stay here. I'm going to get you some clothes." He pointed at the two of them. "Clean up." He left.

"I don't like this," Maria said. "Are you sure this is what you want?"

Ten closed his eyes and saw Amy the instant he did so. "Yes," he said. "But not just for Amy, for everyone. No one should have such a weapon. No one."

"I suppose you're right."

Ten put his backpack in the corner of the room. He took off his shirt. Maria used soap and a washcloth to clean his wound and check to make sure it wasn't infected. "You're good to go," she said.

Ten showered first and threw on a robe that was hanging in the bathroom. Maria was next. She stayed in there a long time and came out wearing a towel. She stood near the mirror that hung over the dresser.

The room was quaint, with a flower motif. The wallpaper was littered with sunflowers, there were photos of flowers and framed botanical drawings from decades past. Fake flowers of various types sat in vases and jars around the room. Even the bedspread and pillows had flowers on them.

Ten knew little about flowers but recognized many of them from flowers that grew in the yards of his old neighborhood.

Ben came into the room holding a huge bag of new clothes. "I guessed for you," he said to Ten. Then he turned to Maria. "But I know your sizes."

She smiled at him.

"Let's get ready. We'll wait until it starts to get dark. The hotel will be busier. Easier to sneak in." Ben headed for the shower.

Ten and Maria went through the clothes. "He's pretty good at this," Ten said.

"He's very observant."

"You love him?"

"Very much. But all this is a little, I don't know…" She laughed. "Not good for the relationship?"

Ten smiled. "It could bring you closer together."

"I'm still struggling with the lying part of it. He is so convincing."

"I know. I feel the same about Russell, even though I understand. I fear that this is what we have now. For the rest of our lives."

"And how long do you think that might be?"

Ten took a deep breath. "I try not to think about it at all." He laid his clothes out on the bed. Jeans, a blue t-shirt, and a long-sleeved shirt of some thick fabric. He looked over and Maria had a similar but different colored outfit. There was one for Ben too. No suits. "I suggest you don't think about it either."

"Anything can happen," she said.

"Yes, anything."

Chapter 11

Later, Ben went out for food. They didn't talk much. They discussed the names on Ten's list, familiarizing one another with each person's possible involvement in ISTI, and in the invention they believed they had a handle on—nanobots used to create disease rather than cure it. After Ten put the list back into his pocket, Ben's eyes became glued to the news playing on a small television that sat on one of the dressers. He listened for any information about those on the list. "Any small thing," he told them, "could help in finding those who are still missing." At one point, he turned around and said, "Once we hit the first person on your DECISION MAKER list, they're going to know we're up to something. They're going to know that we know something."

"Maybe," Ten said. "Right now, they only know who I was involved with. The first other person, they may chock up to you knowing something. I don't think they'll know about our list until we've hit several people on it."

Ben stared at him for a moment.

"An engineer's mind," Maria said. Ben nodded. "I'm going with that, then." He went back to the television until it got dark outside. Then they took a long walk toward the Hyatt. Ben carried the munitions bag and Ten wouldn't let his backpack out of his sight. Besides, he still had his loaded Glock in there.

The evening air smelled of springtime, a bit humid, cool but not cold. The streets were busier than Ten would have imagined, but then, they were in the States' capitol. The three of them walked into the Hyatt. A crowd of people huddled in small groups around the lobby, just as Ben had suggested. There were a dozen or more people waiting to register, all with suitcases and most wearing suits. The three of them walked around and saw that the bar was full, lots of noise.

"He won't have any bodyguards," Ben said.

"How do you know?" Ten asked.

"My job is to know."

"You've been here before," Maria said as though she knew. But her face looked as though it were a question.

"I wasn't surprised to see him on the list. Never liked him. I swear he meets with all sorts of assholes up there."

"Then you know what suite he's in too, don't you?" Ten asked.

"I should go alone," Ben said.

Ten shook his head and Maria said, "Not on your life."

"We all go," Ten said.

Ben had the look of a man ready to lay down the law, but glanced at Maria and must have changed his mind. "In and out."

Ten shook his head again. "No, you don't. My list, my rules. I want him to answer a few questions first."

"I don't like that idea," Ben said.

Ten headed for the elevators with the other two behind him. "Let's go." A lot of people got inside the elevator, which remained fairly full until over half way up to the top. "I should have known," Ten said.

"Always where it's most private, and always where the nicest suites are," Ben said.

The doors opened to an alcove with a table and mirror. Ten got to see the three of them together. They didn't look menacing at all. Ben and Maria really did look like a couple. He could imagine them on a cruise somewhere, or vacationing in Hawaii. He looked like a third wheel, the cousin who saw them and then started to bum around with them because he had no one else to hang with. The image was unsettling. It made him feel lonely.

Around the corner, the hall carpet looked as though it was seldom used. Artwork hung on the walls, some abstract, some natural scenes with trees and fields. The wall colors were pleasant and subdued, unlike some of the other, more flamboyant parts of the hotel. It was a nice hotel, of course, but it was almost as though no one ever used this floor. Ben took the lead. They walked down the hall and around a corner. He stopped in front of a suite, bent down, and unzipped his bag. He pulled out a handgun and silencer, which he placed onto the handgun's barrel. He motioned for them to step back, then shot the lock. He grabbed his bag and went in first. Ten and Maria followed, bent over as though ready to jump or run if they had to.

The suite was larger than Ten's first apartment out of college. He stood straight and walked around. When he rounded a corner, Eric Webber sat in a king-sized bed. He had ear buds in. He reached up and pulled on the cord and they both popped out of his ears. "What the hell are you doing in here? Who are you? You're not from the agency."

Ten walked right over to the bed and pulled the backpack from his shoulder and set it at the bottom of the bed. He unzipped its main compartment.

Eric watched for a moment, then bent to the side and reached for the phone.

Ten pulled his Glock from his backpack and pointed it at Eric. "I wouldn't do that."

Eric went back to his seated position and stared at Ten. "What do you want?"

Ben and Maria must have heard the talking and entered that area of the suite behind Ten. He heard them. Ben stepped beside him.

Eric smiled. "Ben, thank God you're here. I didn't know they were sending you over, but I could have guessed." He pointed at Ten and started to lean forward. "Was this some kind of joke? Not so funny."

Ben pulled his pistol with the silencer from around his back. "You'll want to use this." He took Ten's gun and put his pistol in Ten's hand.

"I don't get this. Ben?" Eric leaned back against the backboard of the bed. His hands shook, Ten noticed. But then, Ten's hands were shaking too. He took a deep breath and tried to let the air out slowly, tried to ease his shaking. He gritted his teeth. "Well?" Eric said impatiently. "What's this about?"

"I'm Tempest Nesbit," Ten said. "You ordered me dead, along with my family." He felt his lips twitch and his eyes narrow. "My wife… my wife was pregnant."

"I don't know you," Eric said, but Ten could tell he was lying. He shook his head and shrugged his shoulders.

"You ordered it," Ten said.

Ben and Maria stayed completely silent.

"I sign a lot of orders. Look, I'm sorry about you and your family. I didn't know. You've got to believe that."

"You knew about the research ISTI followed," Ten said. He shook the gun toward Eric and screamed, "You knew!"

"There's too much research. It's going on everywhere. Really, I don't know individual projects. I report what I know to the president."

"Nanobots? Disease control?" Ten could hardly keep the gun barrel aimed at Eric, his hands shook so much. And now, his mind felt confused. He took another breath, then shook the gun at Eric again.

"These things happen," Eric said.

From behind Ten, he heard someone say, "What the hell."

He swung around. Maria had wandered into a corner near a window with her back to the rest of them and her hands over her eyes. Ben had the Glock, but it was too late. Three men came into the room with guns raised. One pointed at Maria. Ben lowered his hand. Two more men came in behind the first three. Ten lowered his gun onto the bed. He thought it was over for him. He'd taken care of one, only one, but that was enough. He was ready to die. It might even be better for him in the long run. He wasn't sure he could even pull the trigger on Eric.

Eric threw his legs over the edge of the bed and got up. "Glad you guys showed up." He waved his hand toward Ten. "Nesbit, right?" He smiled. "I did recognize you." Then he waved a hand toward Maria. "Dr. Tanner." He walked up to Ben, right in his face. "I can't believe you. You had orders."

"What do you want us to do?" one of the men asked.

Eric shrugged. "Get rid of them. But don't do it here, of course. Get them the hell out of here."

"Sorry, Ben," one of the men said as the five of them ushered the three intruders out of Eric's bedroom.

"I know, Stan. I know." Ben put his arm around Maria's shoulder. Ten followed. One of the other men grabbed the pistol with the silencer, stuffed it into Ten's backpack, and threw it over his shoulder.

Another man grabbed the Glock and Ben's munitions bag. He hefted it a few times and said, "This thing is loaded."

The eight of them stepped into the elevator. "You know the drill, Ben."

Ben shook his head. "Just do as they say." Neither Maria nor Ten argued.

Outside the hotel, there was a police van waiting. The three of them entered the van and sat in seats along one side. Three agents sat across from them, while the other two headed to the front of the van. Doors slammed, the van started, and they were off.

"You're still with Webber, I see," Ben said to Stan.

"A long time," Stan said. "What's with you? All this for sex." He pointed at Maria, who never even lifted her eyes.

Ten watched how uninterested the men were on the ride. One was texting, the other just leaned back and stared at the ceiling. Stan's attention was on Ben.

There was only one thing Ten thought he could do. Fight back. He would probably end up dead either way. Somehow that whole idea of being on a hit list of any sort did something to his courage gene. He had nothing to lose if his life was already on the chopping block. The road was fairly smooth. He waited for the most opportune time, or when it felt right.

"You taking us to the police station?" Ben asked.

"Not on your life," Stan said. "We borrowed this. We've got other plans. I'm sorry, Benny, but you were too soft for all this anyway."

So they were taking them somewhere they could kill them. No police station, no headquarters, nothing like that. Ten listened a little while longer while Stan belittled Ben, then made his move.

CHAPTER 1 2

Ten slid from his bench seat, pushed outward and landed his knees on the feet of the man in front of him. When the man leaned forward, Ten headbutted him. At the same time, he threw a quick neck punch at the other man, who bent over choking.

Ben was no slouch either. He rammed both his fists into Stan's chest, knocking the wind from him, then stood and kneed Stan in the jaw, dropping him instantly. "Idiots," Ben said. He removed the guns from all their captors and emptied the bullets onto the floor.

He reached for his munitions bag while Ten grabbed his backpack. There was a small window in the rear of the van. Ben looked out. "Out of town," he said.

"No comms?" Ten asked.

Ben patted Stan down, shook his head at Ten. "You're right, they are a little arrogant at the moment. I'm sure they'll up their ante when they find we're on the loose again."

"You think they're working with fewer people?"

"Maybe, but that shouldn't stop them from having the right gear. Then again, something might be up."

Maria still hadn't said anything, nor had she moved. When Ben reached for her, she pulled away.

"Sweetie," he pleaded.

"I don't know how long I can do this. Let them have me."

"You don't mean that," he said.

She had tears in her eyes. "I just wanted to do my research, discover something important."

From a crouched position, Ten reached out and touched her shoulder. She turned to look at him. "You did discover something important," he said. "You were involved in one of the most important discoveries of the ages. But like anything invented, it can be used for good or evil. I know that sounds trite, but it's true. The discovery is neutral. But if the wrong people get to use it, we're in trouble. You've got to see that. I know this is difficult, but we have to save… everyone we can."

Maria took a deep breath. She nodded, then reached for Ben's hand. "This isn't easy for me."

"I know, babe. I'll protect you." Ben pulled Ten's Glock from his bag and handed it back to Ten. "Trade you again."

Ten removed the gun with the silencer and handed it to Ben, who removed the silencer and placed it into his bag before zipping it closed.

"We sit on the floor in the middle. Maria, you sit off to the side. We'll shoot our way through."

When the van stopped, Ben and Ten sat on the floor of the van, side by side facing the rear door. The other two men continued a conversation they must have started in the cab. They yelled from either side of the van, came around to the back, and unlocked the door.

Ben shot the second there was the slightest gap in the door. Ten kicked the door open and shot at the second man before he could pull his gun. The two of them jumped from the van and looked around. "We're alone," Ten said.

The area was dark; trees grew all around. The van was still running, its taillights shone red across the dirt road. Exhaust spewed from the muffler. "Not that far outside the city, are we?" Maria said while stepping down from the van. She looked up at the sky. "Still can't see many stars."

Ten stood next to her, rubbing his sore knuckles while Ben frisked the men they'd shot. "You think anyone heard us shooting?"

"We're not going to wait and find out." Ben stood up. He held two guns, which he threw into the trees. Each man had a handful of bullets lying next to him. Ben dragged each of them off the dirt road. "Let's go."

"I'm with you," Ten said.

Maria knelt uncomfortably on the floor of the van as they backed out.

Ten felt a little surprised that he wasn't more upset about shooting the two agents. Was he getting used to this? He hoped not. Maybe he was just tired or desensitized at the moment. He still held the Glock in his hand. He looked at it, could feel its weight, its texture. It had its own smell. He dropped the magazine out and stuffed in a few more rounds, then snapped it back into place.

"Feeling more comfortable with that?" Ben asked.

"No. I hope not anyway."

"You were good back there. What you did. Fast thinking."

"Thanks, Ben. I appreciate that coming from you. But I don't feel so great about it."

"You didn't throw up. That's a good sign. Maybe Russell was right about you." Ben slapped his hand against the steering wheel of the van. "We got to get rid of this thing."

"Where are we?" Ten asked.

"Never been here before." Ben shrugged. "But once I got on the roads, I found signs to the highway. I'm going to drive off one of these upcoming exits in hopes we can find another car to steal."

"We're lucky," Ten said. "A lot of people will be in for the night."

"That's the hope."

"What do we do now?" Maria asked.

"I'm going back to the Hyatt and I'm going to get that bastard," Ben said.

Ten noticed Maria stiffen, then relax, probably on purpose. He didn't relax though. Going back to the hotel didn't sound like the best idea for the night. But then, maybe this was the only window they had. He trusted Ben on that.

It wasn't very difficult to find a car along a street to steal. While getting back onto the highway, Ben asked, "How many cars have you jacked since you started running?"

"Counting this one? Maybe five, six."

"You're pretty good at it."

"My dad taught me when I was really young. He taught me to change an engine and transmission too. Taught me about the electrical system."

"He's a mechanic?"

Ten shook his head. "No. Not at all. He was just interested in everything, mechanics, electrical work, electronics. That's what got me interested. By the time I was in third grade, I'd done more engine work than some mechanics, more electrical repair than some electricians. Even taught me how to solder pipes."

"Sounds like an interesting man," Maria said.

"Yeah, he was." Ten pursed his lips. "He would have loved Amy."

"He died before you met her?" Maria asked.

"Aggressive cancer. Took him in a matter of months."

"What about your mom?"

"Died a few years later. They were inseparable until he died."

"I'm sorry," she said.

"Me too. You know, that's probably part of the reason I got into this field. Who knows? But that's just it, isn't it," he said. "That's the problem here. We're doing our work so that we can save people's lives, so that we can make things better for people. Then some motherfucker, whether the government itself or just parts of this group—the ISTI agency or whatever—anyway, they want to use it as a control, as a way of performing genocide if they choose to, take the choices away from the people. What the hell is that about? Who are these people? This self-appointed control group?" He stopped for a moment. "Sorry about ranting." He slammed a fist on his knee. "I just don't get why the first damned thing people want to do with a new invention, a new cure, is abuse it. Anyone have an idea?"

"There are good and bad people, I guess," Ben suggested.

"Yeah, that about sums it up." Ten fell silent then. He stared out the window as they drove back into DC, parallel parked along the street, then walked a few blocks toward the Hyatt. His nervousness appeared to be over. He noticed that his hands didn't shake and his heart wasn't pumping fast, not yet. Even as they were going up in the elevator, he felt calm. It wasn't until they came to two maintenance men working outside Eric Webber's door that Ten got nervous. Nonetheless, he held out his hand for Ben and Maria to stay behind him as he approached the first man.

"Can I help you?" The man didn't even rise from his job. He remained kneeling at the door.

Ten kneed him in the jaw, and when the other man stood, Ten threw three punches to the man's body and one to the temple. He caught the man before he fell to the floor and placed him flat on the rug. His hand hurt, so he flexed the fingers a few times.

"Only got a few minutes before they're up again," Ben said as he shoved the door open and walked inside. Ten and Maria were right behind him.

Eric sat in the same place he had a few hours before, in his bed with ear buds in and his eyes closed. He must have felt Ben's presence though, because he opened his eyes just as Ben stopped at the base of the bed.

Ten was on his knees unzipping his backpack.

"How the hell did you get back here?" Eric's voice sounded arrogant, not questioning.

"Doesn't matter," Ten said. He rose to his feet with the Glock in his hand, lifted it toward Eric and shot three times into the man's chest.

"What the hell was that?" Ben yelled.

"I was tired of screwing around. Besides, you said we only had a few minutes. It's over. Let's get out of here."

"I hope no one heard that thing go off," Ben said. "I have my silencer, you know."

Ten didn't answer. In the elevator, they stood in silence. Before the doors opened at the bottom floor, Ten said, "That's two."

DIAL IN DEATH

CHAPTER 13

Ben sat in the driver's seat again. The car they'd stolen didn't run very well, so they drove slowly down the highway toward Virginia.

"You know where Metzger lives?" Ten shifted the position backpack between his legs. Darkness closed around the car as they drove farther from the city. The constant rumble of the tires against the road made him feel tired. Ben glanced into the back seat. Ten did the same. Maria was stretched out on her back, her knees bent, her eyes closed.

"We'll get close to his place, nap for an hour or so each, then make our approach," Ben said.

"Won't they be waiting for us this time?"

"You called it before," Ben said. "Could be they still don't realize that you have a list. But he does have a few guards around. Nothing much. Trainees."

"Let's hope so."

"Doesn't matter anyway. We'll do what we have to do."

"You're sounding like me now." Ten lay his head against the seat's headrest. It smelled a bit musty, but not really bad. "You think we'll get killed this time?"

"Morbid question."

"I know." Ten thought for a moment. "Back there when I shot Eric Webber… I felt no remorse. I liked the feeling and hated the feeling. There's something about having your mind set, about doing what you came to do, and another thing about knowing whether it's actually the right thing to do or not. I'm struggling with those two feelings."

"That's the deal," Ben said. "In this business, you sometimes don't know who you're killing or why. You take it on faith that it's the right thing for our country. You forget they're people at all."

"I couldn't kill an animal either. Before this, I mean. It was difficult for me to kill a spider. I used to catch them and let them loose outside. Now…" He thought about Amy saying, *just kill it*. He thought about how she looked nervous when he tried to catch the spider. He felt brave when she acted that way.

He missed her. He missed her a lot.

The car fell silent again. After a few minutes, Ben said, "The last time could be any of the times." He glanced over at Ten and nodded. "You never know, so you have to consider that you won't die. That's all you have in your favor, the knowledge, or the thought, that you won't go down. Sometimes, it's that minor belief that saves you. If you think you might go down, then you might give up."

"Giving up is not an option. I know that. I feel like a cornered rat though. Three cats staring at me. Somehow, I know I won't make it out alive, but my adrenaline won't let me stop fighting."

"That will save your life more often than not." Ben reached over and slapped Ten on the knee. "Get some shut-eye."

Ten relaxed into the seat and closed his eyes for what seemed like only a few minutes. When he raised his wrist to look at his watch, it had been two hours. He sat up. The car was parked off the road in a small dirt turnout. Trees grew all around them. The road wasn't more than fifty feet from them. Ben's head lay back and his eyes were closed. He didn't snore. Maria still lay on her back with her knees up. Her eyes were open. "Hello, sleepyhead." Ten smiled at her and closed his eyes again. The next time he opened them, almost another hour had gone by. He sat upright and leaned near the cracked dashboard.

Ben rolled his head and his neck cracked. Maria sat up. "I'm rested," she said.

Ten opened the car door and stepped into the cool, early morning air. He walked into the woods and behind a tree to relieve himself. When he returned, Maria and Ben stood together talking.

"My turn." Maria bounced away.

Ben walked toward Ten. "We're a few miles away. I'm going to want to walk there, you know."

"I could have guessed." Ten sat on the hood of the car. "How do we make a quick getaway? One of their cars again? Isn't that conspicuous? We'll just have to steal another car shortly down the road."

Ben shrugged. "Okay. Maybe we drive closer. Then we can take this one again. But if they see it, it won't help, and one of their cars would have more guts than this one."

Ten scratched his head, then his chin. He had a few days growth going now and it itched. "Let's go with your original plan. I don't want to ride in this thing any more than we already have."

"Me either," Maria said from behind him. "There's all kinds of trash on the floor back there, and it doesn't smell that good."

"Then we walk," Ben said. They gathered their things and left the car.

Maria appeared in better spirits. "I needed to stretch my legs anyway."

The roadway wasn't very well traveled at that time of night, a few cars drove by, but each time, the three of them jumped into the woods to hide. "This won't be any fun when rush hour hits," Ten said.

"We'll be there by then." Ben motioned toward a path that appeared to go through the woods and started to walk that way. The overhanging branches and thick foliage made it darker in there. "Save us some time," he said.

"How do you know this path? And in the dark, no less." Ten tried to be quiet but had to speak loud enough to get over their footfalls.

Ben stopped and the three of them huddled. "We'll be quiet from now on. But to answer your question: I've protected this place many a time during training. And that's what we have on our side too."

"That you've been here?" Maria asked.

"No," Ten said, "that it's being guarded by trainees."

Ben smiled at him. "You got it." He leaned in to speak quietly. "Here's what we're going to do. When I tap you on the shoulder, Maria, you're going to stay put, lay low, and make no sound." He removed a derringer from his pocket and handed it to her. Then he hefted the munitions bag. "I'll leave this with you too. The derringer has two bullets in it, but you probably won't need them."

She reached for the gun with shaking hands.

Ben nodded toward Ten, who opened his backpack and removed his pistol. He held it up. "I'm ready."

"Once Maria is hidden, you're going to follow me to the rear of the house. There are two sets of sliding doors back there. Easy to break into, just stuff your fingers into the rubber seal and yank. The door will jump its track. I've done it a hundred times. They've never been fixed. After we're in, there are two stairways upstairs to Jacob's bedroom. You take the rear stairs and I'll wind around to the front ones." He held up a finger for Ten to pay closer attention. "There will most likely be only three trainees guarding the house at night. You shouldn't run into any of them. They congregate around the front of the house, both inside and out. I can take them quietly; you can't. Do anything but pull that trigger. It'll put everyone on high alert."

"Not going to be easy," Ten said.

"I've seen you in action. Use the pistol as a set of brass knuckles." He smiled.

Ten couldn't help but smile back and shake his head.

They walked for another few minutes before Ben tapped Maria on the shoulder, dropped the munitions bag next to her, and motioned for Ten to follow him. Ten couldn't believe what they were about to do. He never asked if Jacob Metzger had a wife or kids or a dog or anything. It was like Metzger was the only person in the house at all and that couldn't be true. And those thoughts multiplied. What would happen to Metzger's family once he was dead? What about the kids? Ten worried that his actions could affect the entire family, that the ripple effect could move down family lines for generations. Yet, on the other hand, Metzger was one of the DECISION MAKERS on Russell's list. It had to be done.

Ben moved quickly through the woods and into the open from the side of the house. There were no lights on anywhere. He dropped to the ground and Ten did the same. Ben pointed and Ten saw two men talking in the front yard. He wasn't close enough to hear what they said.

Ben crawled back into the woods with Ten behind him. The two of them rounded the house the best they could from the woods, but eventually had to get into the open. Ben went first, but as soon as Ten stepped from the woods, he heard someone behind him.

"You can stop right there," the man said.

Ten raised his hands, still holding to the Glock. Ben did the same, his gun still in his hand too.

"Drop them," the man said; both guns fell to the ground. "Now walk away, toward the house." They walked about ten feet when the man behind them said, "Stop."

Ten glanced over his shoulder while the man picked up their guns. In front of them, the other two men came around the corner and approached. As they got closer, one of them recognized Ben.

"Ben? What are you doing sneaking around here?"

Ben lowered his hands. "New assignment."

"You're not testing us, are you? If so, Sammy won the prize." The man laughed and pointed to his friend standing behind Ben and Ten.

"More important than testing you," Ben said. "Although," he turned toward Sammy, "you did a great job back there."

"Good thing you didn't try to use these, or you'd be dead," Sammy said about their guns. "Doesn't seem like a very smart way to run a test, to me."

"I told you, it's more important than that. We believe that Jacob's a phony, a stand-in."

"You mean a look-alike?" said the man who knew Ben.

"Bob, this is my new partner, Ten."

Ten lowered his arms and shook hands with Bob.

"Like the number?"

"Stands for Tempest Eugene Nesbit," Ten said.

Ben turned to him and said, "Jesus, you could have come up with something better than that."

When everyone turned with confused looks toward Ben, he punched Bob hard across the jaw.

It took Ten a second to figure out what was going on, and by then, Sammy kicked him in the back of his knees and he went down. No problem; he turned and used both his fists to ram into Sammy's knee, forcing it backward. Now, he went down, both guns fell from his hand, and Ten grabbed the one with the silencer and yelled, "Enough!" Everyone stopped fighting. "Now, you guys lie down together." He slid back from where he was.

Ben picked up the Glock and kicked Sammy's gun away from him.

Ten stood. "You watch them. I'm going after Metzger."

CHAPTER 14

Ben shook his head. "I'm better qualified."

"I'm more pissed off," Ten said while walking away. Ten wasn't going to let Ben stop him from doing what he came to do. He wondered about it though. Was he starting to enjoy the kill? But, no, he couldn't be. He didn't just shoot those other agents. He had no interest in that at all. So was it revenge? Perhaps. He knew that wasn't a positive emotion either, but it could very well be the truth.

He scurried around to the back of the mansion. The lights from a pool flashed across the rear of the house as though it was on fire. Just as Ben had said, two sets of sliding doors led into the house. Ten set his pistol on the ground reluctantly. He didn't want it out of his hand for some reason. Then he placed his head near the door, crammed his fingers into the seal around it, and yanked it from its track. It made a loud clunk. He shoved hard until the door scraped and slid open enough for him to slip inside. He reached out and picked up his gun, then turned into the house. He had to let his eyes adjust from the glowing pool lights outside. Once they adjusted, he spotted stairs just outside the room he was in. Past the stairs was a short hallway near the foyer, which probably lead toward the kitchen and out a back door. He'd remember that as an exit route.

Ten tiptoed into the foyer and toward the front of the stairs when he heard someone speak from a side room located in the front of the house. "In here. I'm sure you're looking for me."

"Metzger?" Ten swung around and walked into the den. A dark figure sat behind a large desk, closed blinds behind him, a slight amount of light as backdrop through the blinds. He couldn't see if the figure held a gun or not. Not yet anyway.

"I got the call about Eric Webber only an hour and a half ago. I told them I didn't need any additional guards, but it appears I was wrong. You found your way in."

Ten took a few resistant steps into the den, then stopped on weak legs. The gun didn't even point at Jacob Metzger.

"You can put the gun down."

Ten bent over and placed the gun on the floor, still unsure if Jacob held a gun.

"Who are you?"

"Tempest Eugene Nesbit."

The dark figure shook his head. "I don't know who that is. Why are you killing people?"

"ISTI."

"What about it?"

"You killed my wife… and dog. You burned my house down, blew up my friend's car."

"You're part of the project, then. Sorry, I seldom heard anyone's name. It wasn't in my best interest to know."

"So you didn't have to be emotionally involved when you pulled the trigger on their lives?" Ten took another step forward. "I'm going to stop you from ever doing that again."

"There are more men willing to make those decisions after I'm gone. You can't stop this, no one can." The mission chief leaned forward and, based on the minimal backlight from the front window, Ten noticed that, as the silhouette of Jacob's hands moved through the air, his hands were empty. He held no gun.

Ten contemplated picking up the Glock he had set on the floor and shooting Jacob, but the conversation wasn't over. He could wait. He longed for information. "Why kill everyone involved?" His voice squeaked as he asked the question; his heart sunk as the image of Amy flashed across his mind. His muscles tensed. Lucky for Jacob, Ten didn't still hold the pistol or he would be dead by now. Interesting how one question could cause such a reaction.

"To keep the technology to ourselves. It'll take years, we anticipate anyway, for the project to be redesigned." He took a deep breath. "I'm sorry about your family." He sounded sorry. "But what you're doing won't help. The technology has already been transferred into the hands of the government. From what I understand, the next step is already underway. Almost every person entering a hospital for any reason, anyone who gets a shot, a pill, surgery, anyone who is born; they're all being injected with nanobots. You can't stop this."

Ten stood transfixed for a moment. The utter scope of the project was ridiculous. Unbelievable. Impossible. Not that big. Not that quickly. It took a moment for the information to sink in. "No." He shook his head.

"You can't stop anything," the mission chief said. "And we'll get you and kill you eventually." The man opened a drawer and reached inside.

Ten dropped to the floor, but was too slow. He felt the bullet go into his shoulder. This one didn't burn like the scratch he'd received before. Ten rolled toward the desk as Jacob stood, most likely to get a better shot, then kicked with both feet against the front edge of the desk, toppling it onto Jacob, pushing him back against the window. Another shot rang out, but Ten didn't wait for a third; he scurried toward the door, grabbing his Glock on the way, and dived into the hall, landing on his wounded shoulder. It nearly knocked the wind from him. He grabbed his arm and ran.

Jacob yelled from the den, "I've already called backup, you idiot!" Another shot rang out, but Ten didn't see where it landed. He rushed straight down the hall, through the kitchen, and out the back door—his escape route.

The sound of a helicopter penetrated his ears. When he looked up, the searchlight roamed far to the right of him, near where Ben held the guards captive. Ten held his arm and ran around the corner. The searchlight landed on the three guards, but Ben was gone. Ten took off in the opposite direction and easily made it into the woods where he could take a circuitous route to where Maria had been stationed earlier. He wished he'd just shot Jacob the moment he'd seen him.

But the information... the information!

He felt a knot grow in his abdomen and work its way up to his throat. Vomit came into his mouth and he swallowed. The thought of what the government could do was horrific. The unlimited control, the insane ability for the government to dial-in death. How could he and his two associates stop such an all-encompassing plan? What could he possibly do?

The helicopter continued to search the area. Now more than ever, Ten wanted back into the house. Kill one more of them, any one of them, just to make a dent, just to show them that they're wrong, what they're doing is wrong. He brushed his sleeve across his wet forehead. He hadn't noticed how much he was sweating or how much he was bleeding. His blood-wet sleeve felt heavy. After a few very long and very slow deep breaths, Ten closed his eyes for a moment. Metzger could have been bluffing. Maybe there was still a chance to stop the plan from happening. Maybe being alive, for now, meant a possibility to stop this was still present.

He hefted the Glock in his hand. Then, knowing that the noise from the helicopter would block the noise from his progress, he moved as quickly as possible through the darkness of the woods. He held his wounded arm. Morning light would be along soon enough, and he had to find Ben and Maria and get the hell out of there. He couldn't help wonder if Ben was the best man to have gone after Jacob, but it was too late. What's done is done, he thought.

In only a few minutes, Ten came to the place where he believed Maria had been told to stay low, but he couldn't be sure. He searched for her, and even whispered loudly for her, but no one answered. He traveled farther into the woods. Based on the sound of the rotors, he looked through the trees and noticed the helicopter had landed. He snuck toward the edge of the woods and saw several men with what looked like machine guns get out of the copter. He shoved back into the woods.

If he couldn't find his friends, then what?

CHAPTER 15

Ten scrambled to get as far away from the mansion as possible. Eventually, he found the path they had come through the woods on, and followed it toward the road where they had left the car. His arm hurt, but the bleeding appeared to have stopped. There was no time to check for sure. He was alone. How would he get out of this one?

In the distance, he heard the helicopter rotors speed up and assumed it took to the sky again. He ducked down in case it was possible for them to see him and continued toward where he'd originally entered from the road. Before he reached the road, Ben stepped from behind a tree. "Figured you'd come this way."

"It's the only way I knew."

"Good enough." He pointed and started walking. Maria held one hand, while Ben carried the backpack over his shoulder and the munitions bag in his other hand. "I'm hoping they don't know about the stolen car just yet. Either way, we'll have to take our chances, change cars as soon as we can."

Maria jumped into the back seat beside Ten and immediately went to his shoulder. "More than a scratch this time, but not much more. You're pretty lucky. It did take a big chunk from your shoulder though."

Ten didn't like the sound of that. "I don't feel lucky."

"You could be dead," Ben said.

"No one else has gotten hurt yet. The bullets keep getting closer to my heart. That's not luck, that's torture."

"You're the one who continues to take risks, knowing you're not an expert." The car jerked forward and Maria stilled for a moment. Ben made a U-turn and headed away from the mansion. "I'll dress this the best I can," she said.

"You should have gone in," Ten admitted to Ben.

"Too late to worry about that. Every situation is different. Keep your mind on the moment; we've got to stay alert, decide what's next," Ben said.

"I failed this time. They're going to be ready for us every step of the way now." Ten cringed as Maria used a water bottle and some old napkins she'd found on the floor of the car to wipe his arm clean. "Is that sanitary?"

"Best we have. Remove your shirt and I'll use it as a compress the best I can."

Ten struggled out of his shirt with Maria's help. His t-shirt had also soaked up a fair amount of blood, but she just rolled the sleeve to his neck and armpit. Then she ripped the bloodied sleeve from his dress shirt and threw it on the floor with the rest of the trash. She ripped the other sleeve off and placed it beside her, then folded the rest of the shirt into a square. Using the clean sleeve, she placed the folded compress over his shoulder, unrolled the t-shirt over it the best she could, and tied the sleeve around his shoulder. "Now stay still for a while. It's seeping, but I think it'll be okay."

"Doesn't feel okay."

"What happened in there?" Ben asked.

"He was waiting for me in the den. I couldn't see."

"Surprised he didn't kill you at that range."

Ten thought about the situation, how Metzger waited without a gun, then went into a drawer for one. Did he have his own death wish? "Me too. Maybe he wasn't sure what to do."

"Self-preservation usually kicks in," Ben said.

"I don't know then. I can only imagine."

"We heard more than one shot," Ben said.

"Three," Maria clarified.

"Only the first one hit. I dived for his desk and tipped it onto him; that's when the second shot went off. Then I ran for the hallway and heard the third shot behind me. He never left the den though."

"You had your gun," Ben said. "He was too afraid to follow you."

"And he'd already called for backup. He yelled it down the hall after me."

"The helicopter." Ben swerved onto the highway. "Next exit."

"Yeah, the helicopter. I saw a bunch of men get out holding machine guns."

Maria reached over the seat and placed her hand on Ben's shoulder. To Ten, she still had that look of confusion on her face, as though she wasn't sure if she was even there at all. She was definitely out of her comfort zone. When she turned back toward Ten, she asked, "Did anything else happen?"

Ten looked away, holding his hand to his shoulder. The pain had increased for a while and now was numbing somewhat. As long as he stayed relatively still.

"Ten?"

"Yeah. We talked. He said that they've already begun to install the nanos into people, the general public."

"Oh my God." Her hand went to her mouth.

"From newborns to anyone getting a shot or pill."

"I know who worked on those delivery systems," she said.

"Could they do this as fast as he says?" Ten wanted to know.

"Maybe. That was handled by Zephyr Biomedical. Gary Satterfield was my contact there."

Ben turned his head toward them. "I'll guarantee they've been preparing for this moment longer than you two have been working on the project. I'll bet my rosy ass they've been geared up for years. I'll bet everything was verified and tried before they declared war on you."

"Then what do we do?" Ten asked.

"Your call," Ben said as he pulled off the highway and into a large parking lot. He jumped out, selected a car, and asked if Ten could start it.

Ten nodded. "Nicer than most," he said.

"We deserve it," Ben said. "You drive," he told Maria.

Ben broke in, then stepped back so that Ten could kneel and reach under the dash. Ben started to walk toward the car they'd just parked. "Forget something?" Ten yelled over his shoulder.

Ben pulled out his pistol with the silencer and shot a hole into the car's gas tank.

The car started. Ten jumped up. "What the hell are you doing?"

Maria slid behind the driver's seat and put the car into reverse and backed out of the spot it was in and away from the car with a hole in its gas tank.

Ten glanced around at the half empty lot. There were no pedestrians anywhere; everyone appeared to be inside. Nonetheless, there must have been cameras. He searched the light poles that stood around and spotted one. "Jesus," he said. "We're being watched, you know."

Ben grabbed his bag and handed it to Ten, who threw everything into the back seat before getting in himself, holding his shoulder. Ben plopped into the passenger seat next to Maria. "Get me closer," Ben said. He pulled out a book of matches, lit one, then lit the entire pack. Flames flared up from his hand. As Maria drove past the car they had just parked, he threw the lighted pack toward a growing puddle of gasoline and a *whoosh* of fire shot from the ground. "Get us out of here."

Maria raced toward the exit and turned right, the easiest turn. The car they left behind blazed in the parking lot as they drove away.

"Next exit, we trade cars again, then a third time before we head in another direction."

Ten saw how Ben was getting their followers off balance. A couple of false starts. Each car owner would call in earlier or later than another one and whoever followed the progress might not know what direction they were actually traveling. Good move.

They stole five different cars before midnight. Ben had Maria zig-zagging in such a way that Ten didn't even know where they were finally headed. Several times before dark a helicopter flew overhead, but never did it appear to follow them. "Do you have a plan?" Ten finally asked.

"You're supposed to come up with that, remember?" Ben said. "I'm just the heavy."

Ten laughed when he called himself *the heavy*.

"He means it," Maria said.

"I suppose he does." Ten leaned back and took a deep breath. He couldn't imagine what he could do, couldn't picture what anyone could do at this stage. They'd won. The government, if that's who was in control, already had a bigger plan than anything he could come up with. They were already underway with their plan too. Ten leaned forward between the front seats. "What can we do?"

"Close your eyes," Maria said.

"What?"

"Close them." Ten did as she asked. He felt her hand on his forearm. She tightened her grip slightly. "Now," she said in the softest voice, "think of your family. I know," she said, "I know, but think of them. Your daughter or son, maybe one of each, and Amy. Think of them. What if they had already been injected? What would stop you from figuring out a way to save them?"

"Nothing," Ten said without thinking about it.

"Exactly."

Her hand left his forearm and he felt her fingers brush a tear from the corner of his eye. "Sit back. And figure this out. I know you can."

Chapter 16

Ten half expected Ben to be heading back toward Metzger's mansion. He'd circled back around before, for Eric Webber. But they were headed toward New York City and Ten knew who was there: Jasper Ignato, the head of International Security for Technical Innovations. He couldn't help but wonder if the group was as frail as it appeared, slapped together for this one project. But if that were the case, perhaps they could crack it completely open. Ten took a deep breath. But what would that matter? What would it matter if they killed everyone in ISTI? The government had already started their plan. No one would be safe. No one.

"I hear a lot of sighing going on back there," Maria said.

Ten's arm didn't hurt as long as he stayed relatively still. His head lay against the headrest. He turned his neck so he could stare out the window and watch the world go by in a rush—cars, trees, buildings, the early morning sky opening. "Can we stop to eat?"

"Drive through," Ben said.

"I don't care. I just need food." Ten yanked a few twenties from his wallet and noticed his arm didn't protest too much. He handed the money to Maria. In twenty minutes, they pulled off an exit, found a Burger King, and were back on the highway. Ten ate his fist-sized burger with gusto. It tasted good.

"So?" Ben questioned.

Ten spoke through a full mouth. "We have to find the other scientists."

"What if they're dead, like Sharon?" Ben didn't mince words.

"Then they're dead," Ten said. "All I know is that killing those on the DECISION MAKING list won't save any additional lives. It'll only avenge those already dead. As much as I'd like to see these people cut into bits and mailed to Alaska, it's the wrong thing to do."

"On several levels," Maria said quietly.

Ten agreed. "Maybe it wasn't like me to go on a killing spree anyway. Maybe my anger just took a few days to subside."

Ben wiggled in his seat and sat forward, hunched over the steering wheel. "I get that."

"But…" Maria said.

Ben reached over and patted her thigh. "If it had been you…"

"Don't make bad matters worse," she said. "Promise you won't do that?"

"You sound as though they've already killed you," Ten said.

Maria stared at Ben as she spoke. "They won't stop until they get all of us. Whatever happens, let's not make this worse. Let's not cause more bloodshed."

Ten recalled how good it felt to shoot Eric Webber and wondered how much of his talk was logic and not emotion. What might he do if swept up in the emotion again? But he heard her loud and clear. He nodded.

Ben didn't make a move. Ten knew that he wasn't making any promises. If they got to Maria before they got to Ben, Ten figured they'd better watch out.

Instead of addressing the conversation at hand, Ben changed the subject. "We don't know who to go after first. There are three of them. If I recall, one's in Oregon, one Seattle, and one in Missouri. None are close, and it would take weeks to find just one of them, even if we knew they were alive. They'll all be hiding." He shook his head while talking, as though none of it worked for him, like he couldn't fathom any of it working out.

"When do they stop looking for us?" Ten asked.

"Never."

"But they've got to slow down. Somewhere along the line, they've got to know that we can't stop them. That we don't matter anymore." Ten just didn't get why ISTI wouldn't just forget about them.

"You can still go to a second buyer," Maria said. Ben didn't have to say it. "Do you have any idea how many of our drugs, serums, pills, etc. are manufactured out of the country, or have foreign shareholders? With something like this, everyone is vulnerable to everyone else."

"Unless…" Ten sat up in his seat.

"We're listening," Maria said.

"If I understand Roger's bots correctly, there may be a way to code them to disengage completely. They'd essentially be rendered stable." He thought a bit longer. "Or…"

"Two plans. I like this," Ben said.

"If we can get hold of Jacob Sempter at Crocket Point, there might be something we can do with the controller. We might be able to shut them all down somehow. There must be some kind of failsafe built into them. There must."

"You trying to convince yourself or us?" Maria said.

"Ben, will there be any information about who is really alive and who isn't inside ISTI's computer systems? There are only three scientists left. One might be able to change the controller, one the nanobots themselves, and Satterfield… can his knowledge help us at all?" It was a question he hoped Maria could answer.

"Don't forget yourself," she said. "You know all the code sequences. Don't you know how to shut them down?"

"Only partially," Ten said. "But... maybe. If I could see what some of the others were up to, I could kluge something together."

"I know how those switches you designed adhere. I might be able to figure out a way to release them. But that might take a second injection, a second delivery system."

"You know what," Ten said, "any information is good information. We can't give up now."

Ben pulled off the highway, down an exit, into a residential area, and parked the car. He reached over and crumpled the bag their food had come in and threw it onto the floor behind Maria. "Might as well leave your trash." He got out. "We walk through this neighborhood for a while. No cameras that I can see. We'll steal another car in a little while."

Maria held Ben's hand and Ten brought up the rear as they walked down the sidewalk. Ben carried his bag, and Ten his backpack. Maria took off her outer shirt and threw it over Ten's shoulder so the blood didn't show through. "We'll get new clothes soon," she said.

Ben just nodded. He said, "You can break into computer systems?"

"Pretty well," Ten said. "I'm not a pro."

"Maybe we can find out everyone's status. I know how to find the ISTI site, if you can break into it."

"Sounds like a plan."

It wasn't long before Ben angled into a side yard and toward a back door. He didn't wait to be asked. "Empty," he said as he reached into his bag and removed his pistol. The sound was that of a bullet hitting a pillow, a heavy *pffftt* as it splintered the lock. He pushed his way inside and Ten and Maria followed. "Kid's room," he said as he jogged down a short hallway, opening doors as he went. He sat at a desk in a room that looked as though it belonged to a twelve-year-old girl. Posters of pop stars were mixed with posters of cartoon horses. The bedspread had flowers all over it. The room was clean. Ben tapped away at the laptop that sat in the middle of the desk, then got up and stepped out of the way. "Here you go."

Ten wasn't a computer programmer in the higher-level manner that would have helped, but he did remember code, he knew sequences, and a friend had once taught him how to confuse a security system to break into it. In fact, his friend had been arrested in high school for breaking into a local government site belonging to the Navy. As long as the ISTI site wasn't too secure. He laughed.

Ben stepped behind him. "What? You find something?"

"I was just thinking that I hope their site isn't too secure." He shrugged. "Struck me as funny—a security group with an unsecure site."

"So you can't do it?" he asked.

"Don't know." He typed. "If I can come up with a known plaintext based on their server sequencing…" He tried several things. "I've done this a few times. Encryptions are just fun to play with… but… an adaptive chosen-plaintext isn't… and, and…" Ten turned around to look at Ben and Maria. He shook his head. "I can hardly believe this." He turned back around. "Quickly, give me the names of people who might know what's going on, people who may have received an email." He snapped his fingers. "How about Ignato? Is he the right person or too high up? Who's on the ground?"

Ben placed a hand on Ten's shoulder. "Try Carter?"

Ten glanced over his shoulder. "Jimmy?"

"No." Ben laughed. "His name's William. I don't know if his email would be Bill or William, but it has a dot between the first and last—"

"Got it. Let me see." Ten created a search and found what he was looking for.

"That's your name," Maria said.

"I know."

"But we know you're alive," she said.

Ben tapped Ten's shoulder. "Good move."

"What?" she asked.

"He's checking the truth of the conversation. If it says that he's alive, then it's internal information, unlike the news media calling him dead."

Ten was far ahead of them now. He let them discuss what he was doing while he forged forward. "Gary's dead." He tapped away. "And…"

"Sempter?" Maria said. She must have been reading over his shoulder.

"Alive," Ten said with a grin.

"What about Roger Floramo at Practical Robotics?" Ben asked.

Ten turned around. "Still missing. We've got two choices. Who first?" He looked at Maria.

"Seattle. If he can disable the nanos, we're home free. No amount of control will be able to operate them."

"Seattle, it is," Ten said. "Now, how do we get there?"

"Close that down," Ben said. He headed out the door.

Ten heard him and Maria walking down the hall toward the back door again. He backed out of the system but hesitated before he hit the last button. Then, he opened a word file, jotted down a few notes and sent it to his own cloud server. Just in case. He shut everything down and rushed to the back door. The others were already outside.

"You look happy," Maria said.

"Never did anything like that before. It felt badass."

Ben laughed at him. "You are badass."

After walking a few more blocks, they stole a car and headed for New York. "We still going after Ignato?" Ten asked.

"I have a friend who can make us fake IDs. We're flying to Seattle this afternoon."

Chapter 17

In a small ranch-style home in New Rochelle, a thin, older man Ben called McGregor led them down a dark hallway into a room the size of a large closet. In a matter of minutes, their pictures were taken and their IDs fabricated. Maria took twenty minutes to clean Ten's wound, which didn't look so bad under the blood-soaked shirt. By the end of her work, the pain had numbed. McGregor's well-equipped bathroom included gauze and disinfecting ointments of all kinds. By the time she was through, Ten felt satisfied with how the wound was healing.

Maria shooed him out so that she could take a shower.

McGregor found a clean shirt for Ten to wear, then he and Ben wandered into the kitchen to talk shop. Ten stared out the window onto McGregor's small front yard for a long while, then wandered into the kitchen where the two men sat together at a short counter, each holding a cup with both hands as though trying to stay warm. Ten smelled tea. Once he entered, they changed the subject.

"Can't thank you enough," Ben said to McGregor.

"Least I can do," McGregor said with a smile before turning toward Ten. "Want some tea?"

"No thanks." Ten never asked what their connection was. He didn't want to know. He hoped that the less he knew, the less reason ISTI would have to stay on his tail. He was probably wrong, but the idea made him feel better.

Ben briefed Ten on how they would proceed. The one thing Ten didn't like was they were going to leave their weapons behind. "McGregor can ship them," Ben told Ten. "Or not. I'll make that decision when I have to."

"How do we protect ourselves?"

"Stay out of the way of trouble."

"Can I take my backpack?"

"Leave it. If we have to get away, it'll be good not to be weighed down." Ben got up and walked toward Ten. He slapped Ten's back lightly as he passed, taking his tea with him toward the bathroom. He showered after Maria got out.

"Join me?" McGregor asked.

"I don't drink tea," Ten said.

"I can make coffee."

"No need." Ten sat across from McGregor. The man's eyes looked older than his thin body. When he smiled, his entire face appeared to grow wider. "This is a very kind thing for you to do."

"Thank you." McGregor made no attempt to explain anything, probably his training, his background. He drank from his teacup and said he was sorry about Ten's wife.

Maria joined them and Ten didn't get a chance to say much about it. After Ben came back from the shower, Ten walked down the hall into the bathroom and washed up at the sink the best he could. Maria didn't want him messing with her handiwork on his shoulder. After he finished, he found the three of them in the living room. McGregor handed Maria a Day-Glo green purse, Ben wore a bright Hawaiian shirt, and Ten was handed a Teamsters baseball cap. He shook it in front of him. "And what's this for?"

"You're getting scruffy. It suits your look," McGregor said.

"Trust him. He's the best," Ben said.

McGregor looked them over, cocked his head to the side, and nodded his approval. "The idea is to have something on you, something that draws attention. That way anyone looking for you won't really see your face."

"You mean like security at the airport?" Ten asked.

"Exactly. Agents are more difficult to fool, as you can imagine, but airport security, not so much. Even if they have photographs, they'll miss the details as they're focused on other things. As your beard comes in, that'll help too. Don't shave for a while and when you do, leave something: goatee, mustache, long sideburns. It'll make you look completely different than you used to." He turned to Ben. "You too." To Maria, he said, "You can always change your hair color."

After they said their goodbyes, the three of them were quickly back on the road toward LaGuardia. Ten fumbled with his ID. "Tennyson Blevins," he said out loud as he read it.

"McGregor likes to be sure you don't have to learn a new name just to be incognito," Ben explained.

"Ten," Ten said.

"Exactly. And I'm Benjamin Carpenter."

"What's your real name?"

"Harper, Ben Harper."

"And you?" Ten asked Maria.

"Maria Palermo."

"Clever."

"He's an expert, as you could probably tell. Any agent worth his salt would recognize when you struggled to talk with one another and had to fumble over one another's name. It would cause them to pay closer attention to additional details. This way, we address each other like we normally would. Easy."

"And they'll pay attention to our accessories instead of our faces," Ten said, carrying the thought through.

"Trust him."

"If you trust him, I do," Ten said. "And what about tickets to Seattle. You think it'll be easy to get flights?"

Ben shrugged. He reached into his pocket and removed several sheets of folded paper. He handed them back to Ten.

"You already have e-tickets?"

"Everything's under control from this side," Ben said.

"From that side?"

"The undercover side. Once we get to Seattle, we're following you. You know the technology. You know where a scientist might hide. I have no idea what to do with any of this."

"I know," Ten said with a chuckle, "you're just the heavy."

They dropped the car off at airport parking, went through security, and were waiting at the gate. "Too easy," Ten said to Ben and Maria.

"Don't think about it. It's not like they've forgotten about you. I'm sure you're still on their hit list."

"Thanks for that," Ten said.

"Isn't that what you were worried about?"

Ten noticed how Ben glanced around nervously the entire time they waited for the plane. The banter was simply small talk. Nothing serious. Ben hardly looked at him while they talked. Maria sat near the window overlooking the flight line, her head slumped as though sleeping. Maybe she was. He wouldn't blame her. Of the three of them, she worried the most. Ten thought about how differently she reacted to their predicament. He hardly cared what happened to him. Since the day he found his house on fire, Amy smothered in their bed, he almost wished they would kill him. He moved his shoulder as a reminder of the wound. As long as he didn't have to suffer for very long, he thought. Eventually, Ben excused himself and went to sit with Maria. Ten had stopped listening anyway. He stood until the plane arrived, unloaded, and they began reloading for the trip. New York to Seattle.

The three of them didn't sit together, and Ten was lucky enough to have a window seat where he could stare out during the entire trip, avoid the unwanted chit chat that sometimes happened when two people sat together. He wished McGregor and Ben had let him bring his backpack stuffed with food, but his hands were empty. He waited patiently until the stewardess offered a light meal for eight bucks.

Ben sat in the rear of the plane, then Maria, then Ten closest to the front, but still in row eighteen. The flight was smooth, the food poor, and the company quiet. He felt good about the trip. He let the other passengers in his row get out and just sat there waiting for Maria and Ben. Maria came down the aisle and sat with him. "How was your trip?"

"Same as yours, I suspect."

"Easy, then."

He nodded. A few minutes later, Ben stood over them. Maria got up and waited for Ten to lead. Without luggage, they skipped baggage claim and took the overpass to the parking deck and taxi waiting area. It was easy to get a ride, but they had no idea where to go. Ten asked the cabbie to drop them off downtown at the Hyatt. He figured every town had a Hyatt. In twenty minutes, they were on 6th Avenue. Ten noticed the Space Needle off to the side of the hotel. The sky darkened with the coming night. He paid the cab driver and went inside.

"You're paying cash," Ben said. "Get a suite. One night. We'll come up behind you."

"Got it."

The middle-aged receptionist explained that they had no more suites available. "They're all being used for demonstrations."

"Oh? Then a regular room."

"Two queens good?"

"Sure," he said. His luck had stuck with him. He handed over close to three hundred for the room, after all the local and state taxes.

The receptionist looked surprised when he pulled cash from his wallet. "We usually accept a credit card to secure the bar in the room," she said.

He still had his debit card on him, but it had the wrong name on it. "I'm lucky I have this." He laughed. "The airline lost my luggage, including my wallet and credit cards."

"You packed your credit cards?" she asked, apparently a bit surprised.

"Carry-on," he said. "It had all my stuff. The plane was full and they checked my bag at the last minute. I wasn't thinking."

"Seems odd that they'd lose that one."

"I know." He shrugged. "Look, I'm only here until my sister picks me up in the morning. If I promise I won't touch the bar…"

"I can waive it this time." She handed him the room key and pointed toward the elevators. "Have a pleasant stay."

He nodded and walked toward the elevators. Tomorrow he could try to replenish his cash. It had only been days. His account could still be open. He'd have to come up with a better story, though, next time. As soon as he got on the elevator, Ben and Maria showed up and got on with him. "They wanted my credit card for the in-room bar," he said.

"What'd you tell them?" Maria asked.

"Airline lost my bags."

"And your credit cards were inside your luggage?" She looked as confused as the attendant was earlier.

Ten just shook his head. "I took care of it."

When they stepped inside the room, Ben checked outside the window. Maria stepped next to him and put an arm around him, then leaned her head on his shoulder. "Order room service," Ben said. "The biggest meal they have. We're sharing it."

Ten did as he was told. "You think we're safe here."

"For the night at least." Ben turned around and stared at Ten for a moment.

"What?"

"If you found out that someone was out to kill you, where would you hide?"

"Like that's a real question," Ten said. "I don't know this guy at all. And if he was saved by his bodyguard, then maybe that guy took him somewhere. You'd know better than I would."

"Wouldn't happen. Trust me."

Ten shook his head. "I don't know. Go to the mountains?"

"Sleep on it. You'll have to do better than that in the morning."

CHAPTER 18

Ten slept hard and deep. When he woke, Ben stood over him. The clock said 2:45. "It's early," he mumbled.

"Your turn to stand watch."

"We're in a hotel," Ten reminded him.

"No reason to be clumsy about our safety."

Ten took a deep breath. "You're right." He still wore his pants and t-shirt. He had thrown the comforter over himself. He twisted at his waist and saw that Maria still slept. "Do I need my shoes?" he asked, seeing that Ben still wore his.

"No." Ben backed away from Ten and pointed at the stuffed chair he had placed facing the door. "Don't fall asleep."

"I promise." Ten went to the bathroom, peed, and then washed his hands and threw cold water over his face to wake up more. He felt surprisingly refreshed when he walked out and sat in the chair. He had no weapon, so he didn't know what he'd do even if someone did come by to harm them. He thought about that for a moment and got up and pulled a hangar from the closet. There was an iron in there too, so he grabbed that as well. He placed both next to the chair, sat back, and waited. Ben's breathing deepened in less than three minutes. He probably had to learn how to get to sleep fast in order to do his job.

Ten thought about their next step. If he were Roger, where would he go if someone were out to kill him? He laughed to himself. He was attacked and he went after his attackers. But Roger didn't have the list that he had. Hopefully, his bodyguard helped him escape, but that still didn't provide any clues to where he may have hidden. So, what if there were no list, what would he have done? Hide out, of course, but where?

Ten glanced around the room, thought to pick up something to read, but then just stayed where he was. He'd become pretty bored if he merely hid out somewhere there was no equipment to work with. Plus, he couldn't go anywhere familiar, like a cabin in the woods or anything like that. Where would be a good place? A friend's, but that would put his friend in danger, so no. An abandoned building perhaps? Preferably one with some equipment. A lab. An abandoned lab? Or school. Ten snapped his fingers and heard Ben rustle in bed. At least he didn't wake up.

He grabbed a pen and pad from the desk. He wrote ABANDONED SCHOOL, ABANDONED LAB, GOVERNMENT FACILITIES NO LONGER IN USE, A FAILED TECHNOLOGY COMPANY. Those were the places he thought they should look. Preferably places with microscopes? But anything would work. Roger wouldn't have to be able to continue his nanobot research, he could work with larger items. Ten felt that Roger would want something to do. That's how he'd feel. That's how he felt already, sitting in that chair, in the quiet, in the relative dark. Yeah, he would want to be able to do something, anything.

By the time Ben and Maria got up, Ten had a plan. He didn't know how he'd find the information he wanted, but he'd find it. His best guess was online, of course, which meant they'd have to find a cyber-store somewhere around. There must be one… or a library, of course.

They each took turns showering, and they each complained about having to dress in the same clothes. "We'll buy more today," Ben said to Maria. "I promise."

"While you two are shopping, I'm heading to the library to do some research. We'll find him. I know it."

"After breakfast," Maria said. She had just finished drying her hair using the hotel's hairdryer and stepped around the wall leading to the bathroom.

"Agreed," Ben and Ten said at the same time. They laughed at themselves. "It's nice to lighten the air," Ben said.

At the restaurant, they each ordered a hearty breakfast, three omelets with meat in them. Ben asked for a fruit salad too. Orange juice and coffee all round.

As they were finishing their breakfasts, Ben leaned in and the others followed suit. "We're leaving together and not splitting up."

"I'm going to the library," Ten said.

"We're being watched. If we're followed, we'll have to figure out how to get away or stop him from following us."

"Him?"

"One guy, but I'm not telling you who or you'll both look at him." He tapped his finger on the table. "And don't look around either. Focus right here."

Ten paid in cash. They got up and headed for the lobby and then the front entrance. Ben stood by the door as a porter opened it.

"Still behind us," Ten asked as he walked by.

"Yes. Stay close."

Outside they began to walk up the street. "Wouldn't it be easier if we split up? I could go around the block and come up behind him," Ten said. "You stay with Maria." She hadn't said anything so far, but held to Ben's hand.

"And what?" Ben asked. "You have no weapon."

"But he'll be surrounded."

"Let's see what he does first," Ben said. They crossed the street and Ben turned and waited to cross again. "He's gone."

"You think he's going for reinforcements? Surrounding us?" Ten looked behind them, then up and down the street.

"Stop acting nervous," Ben said.

"But I am nervous."

"Just walk." Before they made it to the end of the block, Ben said, "Here he comes."

"Toward us?"

"Just came around the corner."

A man dressed in a dark suit and muted tie slowed and stopped in front of Ben. "Roger Floramo is safe."

"And you are?" Ten said, stepping closer to the man.

"Something's not right," the man said while removing an ISTI ID that he showed to everyone. "We've never been asked to kill our—"

"You alone?" Ben interrupted.

"Of course." The man looked at Ten and Maria. "But you're not."

"Maria Tanner and Tempest Nesbit," Ben said.

"He's supposed to be dead."

"Well, I'm not," Ten said.

The man looked around. "Let's walk." They headed back toward where they came from, but then took a side street. Ten still didn't know what to think. They could be traveling into a trap. But Ben would know that, right? He couldn't just trust every ISTI agent they ran into. In fact, why should they trust any of them?

The man walked around a car to unlock the door and get in.

"You're not being followed?"

"They think I killed Roger and dumped him into the river. That's what my report said. I've only recently been reassigned. So they'll find out soon, when I don't show up in DC."

"I don't get any of this," Ten said from the back seat.

"None of us do," the man said. He held out his hand toward Ben, who sat up front. "Jake Wright."

"Is he holed up in a lab somewhere?" Ten asked.

"How'd you know?" Jake said.

"Wild guess," Ten said, glad he had guessed right.

"How'd you know we were here?" Ben asked.

Ten noticed that Ben never kept his eyes off of Jake.

"Home office sent me to take you out."

"Just you?" Ten didn't believe him.

"No. There were three of us. I took care of the other two this morning. We can go back and I can show you which dumpster they're in if you like."

"Won't be necessary," Ben said.

Ten noticed the signs for I-5 North when they got on the highway. He also saw that Jake became more nervous the longer Ben stared at him. Was that some kind of tactic? What was going on between them? When he looked over at Maria, she nodded toward the front seat and shrugged. Ten shrugged back. At least he wasn't the only one who noticed the tension.

After about a half hour of driving, Jake broke the silence by asking over his shoulder, "Who told you where Roger was?"

Maybe that's why he was nervous. He didn't trust them.

"That's what I would want," Ten said. "We love our work, and if we're going to hide away, we'd might as well be able to do something."

Jake laughed uncomfortably. "Yep, that's what Roger said." He gave Ben a strained smile.

Ten was beginning to wonder about Jake and where they were going. The car fell silent again. Jake took an exit that Ten didn't notice, then drove into a wooded area, made a few turns, and kept going for another forty minutes. Wherever they were, it was back in the woods somewhere. Ten had tried to keep track, but feared he wouldn't be able to get them back out as easily as they got in. They pulled up outside a fairly bland-looking building that looked more like a vet's office than a government lab. Of course, that would do in a pinch, especially if the lab equipment were still there. Maybe, that is. The place was probably stripped of medicines, fluids, etc. Might be as boring a place as a bare cabin.

"There's a car here," Ten said.

"Roger's."

"You saved him and then drove here separately?" Ten asked.

Before they got out, Ben grabbed Jake by the collar. "Your gun."

Jake looked scared, which made Ten nervous. "It's a trap, isn't it?" Ten said.

Ben opened his door and dragged Jake out of the car and shoved him ahead of them. He held the gun at Jake's back. "Stay in the car!" Ben yelled.

Ten was already out. He motioned for Maria to stay. She quickly climbed between the seats and plopped into the driver's seat. Ten ducked as he walked past and saw that the keys were still in the ignition. Jake didn't have time to remove them.

"Get back there," Ben said.

"Not on your life." Ten stepped next to Ben, but before they got to the door, a window broke and three shots were fired. Ben bent over and Jake ran for the front door, but didn't reach it before Ben shot him in the back of the head. Ben fell to the ground. Ten dropped next to Ben, grabbed the gun, then leapt and dived for the foot of the building, then scurried toward the side. Maria screamed from behind him and he hoped she had the sense to stay in the car with her head down. He heard two more shots, but didn't have time to check on her. He slowed when he neared the rear of the building. If it were a vet's office, there would be several exam rooms along the outside. Could he sneak inside? He looked back the way he'd come. A door slammed out back. He racked the pistol he held and lifted it to his waist, ready to protect himself if he had to.

Ten sat quietly, then stood, peeked around the corner, and a gun was parked close to his face. He didn't hesitate.

As the man behind the gun was telling him to hold still, Ten raised the barrel of the pistol and pulled the trigger. The face of the man standing before him grew into that of complete surprise. Ten raised his other hand and pushed the nose of the man's gun out of his way. Someone inside the house yelled, "You get 'im?"

Ten automatically yelled, "Yeah." When the other man stepped from the back door, Ten shot him twice, then ran for the door. Inside, he yelled for Roger as he walked slowly from one doorway to another. He heard muffled sounds. In one of the exam rooms, Roger lay strapped to a table with a gag in his mouth. Ten removed the gag. "Just three of them?"

"Yeah."

"I'll be back." He ran for the front door, opened it, and yelled for Maria. Her head popped up over the dash. The second she saw him, she threw open the door of the car, and ran toward Ben.

Ten went back inside for Roger. Somehow he knew Ben hadn't made it. Maybe it was how he fell, or that he made no noise. Ten wasn't sure about the why, just about the what.

Game On

CHAPTER 19

After untying Roger, Ten ran out to comfort Maria. She held Ben in her arms and rocked, crying quietly, as though she didn't want anyone to hear. Ten knelt next to her, but didn't move to touch her. He remained quiet until Roger stepped from the building and nodded toward Ben and Maria. "His name's Ben," Ten said. "He was Maria's bodyguard. He's done everything he could to protect us."

"I'm sorry," Roger said. He looked to be middle-aged and stood about the same height as Maria, but carried about forty extra pounds. His eyebrows were dark and thick and met in the middle. His teeth were crooked on the bottom, but not on the top. Ten had never met him before. He didn't look impressive at all.

Maria shook her head, then scooted her legs from under Ben and lowered his head softly onto the ground. She looked up at Ten. "How can we keep this up?"

Ten had no words for her, so he kept silent.

She reached for him and he stood and helped her stand.

"Do you want to be alone?" he asked her.

"I want to stay with him, and yet I want to leave so that I don't have to look at him this way. I don't know what to do." She turned into Ten and he let her rest her head against his shoulder.

"Let's go inside for a little while." Ten led her into the abandoned vet's office. Roger followed them inside. While Maria sat in one of the dusty chairs in the waiting room, staring at the wall as though dumbfounded, Ten and Roger walked toward the back of the building to talk.

It had taken Roger a little while to wrap his head around what had happened. But once he sorted things out and pieced overheard conversations together, he explained what he thought he understood. "I originally thought these guys were just going to kill me. Jake was my bodyguard, I found out. He had posed as a concerned neighbor for the past ten years or so. A long time. I always thought we were friends."

"The other ISTI agents?"

"ISTI?"

"International Security for Technological Innovations."

"If they're part of a government group, then what happened?" Roger obviously didn't understand what he thought he did.

"Big stakes, I suppose." Ten walked over to a counter and leaned his hip against it.

"I heard them say something about holding me until they found at least two of the others. Those two must be you and Maria." He cocked his head. "She's Dr. Tanner. I've seen her picture."

Ten acknowledged he was right. "They must have thought they hit the jackpot when we showed up."

"They were planning on selling us… our knowledge."

"That's what the government was afraid of all along. I suppose if they don't want the problems, they shouldn't do the research." Ten didn't feel very sympathetic at the moment.

Roger stared at Ten. "You think we should check on Maria?"

Ten shook his head. "Ben's dead. She needs to be alone." He walked over to a window. "We should bury him and get out of here."

"Just go," Maria said from the doorway. Ten and Roger turned around to look at her.

"You're going with us," Ten said.

She shook her head, but not convincingly. "Why?"

"Now, more than ever, we're in trouble. I don't know if all this is some inside job and that all these people played ISTI, or once the government realized what we had here, they decided to scrap the project and us with it, or just us? I don't know anything right now. But what I do know is that a lot of people are after us, which most likely means other countries, other governments or factions, know about our research. They'd all love to be in control of this technology. Think of what could happen."

"I have. But we can't get away. It's impossible. Let them kill us," she said. "That's what they're going to do eventually. Someone is. And if we're captured, will we give our secrets away? No," she answered her own question. "So, whatever other government or group captures us will most likely torture us until we die anyway. I'd rather go quickly, at the hands of ISTI. At least, then, our government is the only one with the technology."

"They can't even be trusted," Ten said. "These three were on the team and were going to sell us out. Who do we give up to?"

"I don't think they knew what we were involved with," Roger said out of the blue.

Ten swung around. "What?"

"These three, they just knew that whatever I was researching was important," Roger said.

"Did you hear who they were hoping to sell to?"

"No."

"Hardly matters," Ten said.

He glanced over at Maria. "You okay? You know I won't leave you behind, so I hope you're ready to go."

She shook her head, and walked toward him. Ten met her halfway and she laid her head on his chest and cried. "I loved him."

"I know." It was all there was to be said. "We need to leave before we're found."

She lifted her head. "I've paid my last respects." She glanced at Roger and pushed away from Ten.

Ten knew she didn't want to see Ben lying dead out there. He felt her resolve. She was already a strong woman; the events of the past few days only made her stronger. Either that or apathetic, which wouldn't be good. He hoped it was stronger. He did notice that he killed with more ease, especially after seeing Ben go down. Something had gotten into him. He wasn't about to die and he knew it. He could still see the barrel of that gun in his face and had no idea what made him shoot. There was no thought any longer, just action. He had to rely on instincts.

"Roger, we'll be talking about your work and how we can neutralize those bots." Ten pointed at the man. "Be thinking about that." He reached for Maria and touched her arm for a moment. "I'm going to drive the car around the back. Meet me there." He looked between the two of them. "Grab guns and ammo. Anything you can find. They must have had food here too. Pack it up."

He walked toward the rear of the building and out the back door. He stepped around the body and bent down to remove the man's wallet and extract the cash from inside. Ten patted him down and found his ISTI ID and put it in his own pocket. He didn't find any more bullets, and the gun lying next to the man had only one magazine. He still grabbed the gun and headed for the man he shot at the corner of the building. He made the same thorough check and found similar items. Next, he ran around the side with the three guns in one hand and IDs in the other. At the car, he threw everything onto the passenger side floor. He went back to where Ben lay. He stood over the man for a minute and said a silent prayer. He thanked him for his loyalty toward Maria and his help thus far, then wished him well on his journey to his next life. "Goodbye, my friend." Before he walked back to the car, he retrieved Ben's wallet and ID as well.

In the car, Ten threw Ben's stuff onto the floor with the others'. He started the car and backed far enough to turn the wheel and drive over the grass next to the building. The parking lot had a road that went around a well-groomed park-like area between the front lot and the rear lot, but Ten took the shortcut through the small park.

Maria and Roger waited with several bags and duffels fat with contents. Maria threw her bags into the back seat and then sat up front next to Ten, pushing the guns and IDs out of the way with her feet. He didn't say anything to her, but after she closed the door she said, "I'm better now." He noticed a tightness in her voice. Was it anger? He hoped it wasn't revenge. He knew what that felt like and it was a struggle every moment to keep it under wraps.

As he drove from the lot, he thought about the bigger picture. They had to somehow find a fail-safe button on this technology and shut it down. Forever, if possible.

"We've got to find a mall somewhere and swap cars," Ten said.

"Not this again?" Maria smiled at him, but it was strained.

"I'm afraid so." He kept driving.

CHAPTER 20

Another mall, another car. This time, Ten chose a gray BMW, old, but in good shape. He liked the subdued color and hoped it didn't attract any attention. He continued to drive, working his way south toward Oregon. At one point, he removed the list and handed it back to Roger. "Know anyone on either of those lists?"

"Some."

"Who? How?" Maria asked.

"Well, Satterfield for one. But according to those guys back there, he's dead."

"Did you believe them? Or was it just something they had heard?"

"I believed them. I think one of those guys was Satterfield's bodyguard." Ten saw him crinkle his eyes and face and thought he was going to cry. "Executioners are what we should call them. They probably knew they were going to kill us all along."

"That's not true," Maria said. Ten knew she didn't want to believe that, but then, he didn't believe it either. His own friend, Russell Arden, was no executioner. He was a good friend.

"Maybe not Ben, but Jake was. I should have seen it in him long ago. He had this mean streak, you know. Didn't like cats. Actually poisoned a dog that used to shit in his yard. A real—"

"Enough," Ten said. "Let's concentrate on the situation. You know anyone else on that list? Anyone at all?"

"Of course I recognize the names. Let's see. Here you go; besides Satterfield, I've talked with Senator Cornhill and a few of the guys over at Smithers Pharmaceuticals, but not for this project. Although they did ask some funny questions."

"Probing for information about potential delivery systems I bet. Someone must have informed them you were involved." Ten reached back for the list again and put it into his baggy and back into his pocket. "What about Cornhill? How do you know him?"

"He visited our offices a few times as part of some technology committee he's on, I think. I really don't get involved in politics." Roger reached next to him and unzipped one of the packs and pulled out a banana. "Anyone else hungry?"

Maria held her hand toward him and he placed the banana into it. Ten shook his head. "Not right now. So, did the senator go through your department?"

"Sure. We're doing the coolest stuff."

"Does he know what you do? I mean, the whole multi-purpose nanobot thing? That you discovered how to get them to rearrange for different purposes?"

"Not exactly. How much could he understand anyway? He's a senator, not a scientist." He shrugged. "But then, I don't remember completely. That was a while ago. But a lot of people have a general idea what I'm up to. You can find my research papers all over the internet. I didn't talk about this project, though, not that I know much more about it than my part."

Ten didn't believe him at all. Roger appeared to be the kind to talk, figuring no one understood what he was doing and therefore could never figure it out. For as arrogant as that was, it was wrong. No wonder ISTI wanted them all dead. A couple of people like Roger, with even the slightest knowledge of the technology and what it can do, and there'd be plenty of interested parties. He shook his head while thinking.

"What?" Maria asked him.

"Innovation," Ten said.

"What about it?"

"There is a natural progression to every technology, every idea, every product. Several, in fact. Innovation happens when you have a basic product or technology. It happens in steps, usually in several different directions at once until something clicks, then it takes off primarily in that particular direction. And if it's something to profit from, the intensity of the research increases, and one innovation after another occurs. Same goes with what we're doing. All these technologies merged in a way that innovation was bound to happen. Our government can't stop this. It's a natural progression. We're headed for this technology whether we like it or not, whether we're involved or not. They just wanted us to help jumpstart it, to put them ahead of the game… for now."

"It's all futile, then?" Maria said.

Ten noticed Roger wiping his eyes. Maybe he was crying. "Not futile. Eventually, ISTI or some group like it is going to realize that we're too important to eliminate. We're the only ones, so far, who can recognize this technology and possibly control it, or eliminate it. We can fight back. We're valuable."

"How are you going to get close enough to let them know?" Maria asked. "And how do we know who to trust? Some of these people, we already know, are out to sell us and our knowledge, while others want to eliminate us to get what we know off the market."

"I don't know any answers at the moment, but Roger is going to figure out how to dismantle these things and he's going to teach me and you. And I'm going to teach you what I know and you're going to teach us."

"Transfer of information," Roger said from the back seat, his mouth full of banana. Maria had half eaten hers as well. "Once that starts to happen, they'll only need one of us. Is that smart?"

"It's necessary for us to be able to stop this."

"You're walking a thin line there, Tempest."

"Call me Ten."

"Thin line," Roger repeated. "They'll only need one of us. Only one has to break."

"But one can help save the world," Maria said.

"And they won't know if we passed this onto others or not," Ten said.

"Sounds dangerous on a lot of levels." Roger finished his banana and reached into the bag for something else to eat.

"It's the only way," Ten said.

"I agree," Maria said. "Where can we hole up for a few days?"

"There's a place near Crocket Point," Roger said.

Ten gave him a concerned glance.

Roger smiled broadly. "I suspect since we're headed that way, you're going to try to find Jacob Sempter. I may have a few ideas about that."

"I thought you didn't know him," Maria said.

"Never met him or talked with him, but he's a friend of one of my old college roommates. They spent a lot of time hiking several trails. We just have to find out which one."

"And you can do that?" Maria asked.

"Got a cell phone? I'll call my friend."

Ten pointed to his pack on the floor next to Maria's legs. Several guns sat down there too. "Yeah, in my pack. We might want to put those guns away too."

Maria found the phone and handed it back to Roger. "How do I get the clips out?" Maria asked.

"Magazines," Ten said. "And there's a thumb press button on the grip."

"What are they?" she asked. "They look different than yours."

"Don't know. Mine's a nine millimeter, according to the guy where I got the magazines and rounds."

She started to cry. "Is one of these Ben's?" She let the pistol in her hand drop to the floor.

"I don't remember which one. They're all the same."

She bent and picked one up. "This one, then." She rolled it in her palm.

"Careful."

She dropped the magazine onto the floor. "That better?"

Ten shook his head. "Probably a round in the chamber." He leaned over and pointed at the safety lever. "Let's keep the safety on."

Roger started talking with his friend, but Ten ignored their conversation. He focused on what Maria was doing.

She ejected the round from the chamber and it flew onto her lap. She jumped slightly. "Oh." Then she laughed and looked at Ten. She still had tears on her cheeks. She was all over the place. "Surprised me." She turned back to the next pistol and ran through the same operations.

"Keep mine loaded." Ten held out his hand and she placed his nine millimeter into it. He slid the barrel under his thigh so it didn't slide around.

Maria put all the pistols in the pack.

Roger leaned between the seats. "I'd like one of those. I don't want to be without a weapon."

"You know how to use one."

"Close enough. I've gone to the firing range a few times."

Ten nodded for Maria to hand one back. She gave him one of the extra rounds and one of the magazines. Ten never mentioned checking to see how many rounds were still in it. He wasn't too sure of Roger anyway. "Find anything out?"

"I might know where he is. I can lead you there once we get closer. Just keep heading south on I-5 for a few more hours."

"We'll have to trade cars out a few times… to be safe, I mean." Ten watched for an airport or mall exit. They were always the best places. Lots of cars.

Maria leaned back into her seat with her head angled to look out the window. She held her hand next to her face and her shoulders shook. She wasn't as okay as she made out to be, but Ten could understand that.

It surprised him that he wasn't a complete basket case himself. But then, something inside him compartmentalized everything going on and everything that already happened. He had to go into that particular part of his brain to find the sorrow, and he tried his best not to do that. There were more important things to take care of and right now, that included finding Jacob Sempter.

CHAPTER 21

Somewhere a few miles south of the Oregon border, near Portland, they pulled into a large mall parking lot to exchange cars. Ten pulled through a drive-through ATM and was still able to withdraw money from his account, but got a strange feeling doing so. If ISTI **could** follow him through his bank activities, then he'd have to stop. And now would be a good time. "Wait here," he told the others as he parked the car.

"Why?" Maria asked.

"I'm going to the bank." Ten jumped out and walked into the bank where he filled out a withdrawal slip for three thousand dollars.

When it was his turn at the teller's station, the woman looked at him with suspicion. "I'll need to see your ID, sir."

He pulled out his wallet. "I know this is a lot of money, but my daughter is moving from the dorms into an apartment and I just want her to be comfortable. Help her out," he said.

"Daddy's girl." The teller was in her thirties, pleasant face, and well dressed in a sharp baby blue blouse. "My husband and our daughter are the same way." She turned toward her computer and punched some keys. Then she called for her supervisor to approve the withdrawal. The super glanced at his ID as well, then okayed the transaction.

Ten felt a thickness in his chest as soon as he mentioned his daughter. He had opened the wrong door in his mind and became aware of a catch in his throat. He held back his emotions as the teller counted out three thousand dollars in hundreds. He didn't say thank you for fear his voice would crack. He just nodded politely and walked out. That was it. The last time he'd be using his account. When he got back into the car, he handed five hundred dollars each to the others. "Hold onto this in case you need it. It's all we're going to have for a while." He stuffed a few hundred in each pocket and a wad of bills into his wallet that made it a bit thicker than comfort allowed. He'd be fine.

The other two got out of the car. Maria handed Ten his backpack. When he shouldered it, he felt the hardness of the pistols against his back. Between his backpack and the munitions bag, they seemed to be collecting weapons. Ten walked to the outskirts of the parking lot, Maria and Roger following, and jacked another car.

Just as they were throwing everything inside, a security cop in an electric vehicle pulled up from out of nowhere. "Hey, what the hell are you guys doing?"

Ten glanced at Roger and Maria and shrugged. They should have been watching while he was messing with the wiring. The car, a greenish Dodge Dart, sat running with its doors wide open.

"Would have thought you'd steal something nicer," the young man said as he stepped from his cart.

Roger began to shake and the man turned toward him with a grimace.

Ten stepped forward. "It's my wife's car. She lost her keys and I don't have a set. I just came to help her."

The man cocked his head and walked toward Ten. "You got ID?"

Ten saw Roger pull the pistol from his bag. "No!" Ten yelled.

When the man turned around, Roger pointed the gun at him. "Just leave us alone."

The guard raised his hands and began to sweat from his forehead. "O-o-o-okay. Okay," he stuttered. "It's okay. Don't shoot."

"Don't," Ten said.

"But he saw us," Roger said.

"Cameras." Ten pointed to a light pole. "We're never alone. We just have to keep moving." He couldn't believe he was having to talk down the person he traveled with. "Listen, Roger. You don't want to make things worse."

Maria stepped closer to Roger. "Put it away," she said.

Roger lowered the pistol, but the guard kept his hands in the air. Ten stood behind him. He knew how to knock a man out with a well-placed blow and did so, then caught the guard as he fell. "Move that damned vehicle," he told Roger as he dragged the guard into the grass at the end of the lot.

"How you do that?" Roger asked.

"Don't ask."

Roger moved slowly, but backed the electric security vehicle out of their way before getting into the Dart with the others. Ten backed from the parking space, then left the lot, heading south. "How far?" he said after a few minutes.

"Three or four hours," Roger said. "We're going to Crater Lake Park." Roger appeared to be in a slight daze as he talked. Maria stared out the window. And Ten held back tears as he drove. They exchanged the Dart for a Camry about halfway there. It drove smoother, but the seats were pretty ripped up. It smelled like dogs had lived in it for a long time too. Not the worst smell, but not the best either.

Eventually, Maria suggested they stop and eat.

Ten nodded and took the next exit, but kept driving for a while.

"Where you going?" Maria asked.

"Farther from the highway than usual. I can't imagine how they could be following us, but they have been so far. I don't want to make it too easy." A few more turns and another half hour and Ten pulled into a diner at the edge of Denville, a small town nestled into a valley. It looked as though it might have been larger at one time; empty buildings sat all around the diner and across the street. Only one other store stood open on that block, an antique store with a few old chairs and coffee cans on the sidewalk in front of it, as though the space overflowed onto the street.

The three of them got out of the car. Ten kept his backpack with him all the time. They left the other bags in the car.

A middle-aged woman of about five-three with a dirty apron showed them to a table. Only two other tables were occupied: one with a young couple who looked as though they were arguing, the other with two older men having a jovial discussion, thoroughly enjoying each other. Ten faced the door and Maria sat next to him. Roger slid all the way into the booth next to the front window. "How have we made it this far?" Maria whispered.

"I was just wondering the same thing," Ten said, keeping his voice low as well. "I don't really know the answer to the question though. For me, it's been like some kind of dream. I mean, how many days has it been? Not many. And how many men have we killed? Too many and yet not enough."

"What do you mean, not enough?" Roger leaned in so he could whisper like they were.

"These people killed my wife and unborn child. I meant to hunt each of them down and kill them. I only got to two, so far." He shook his head.

"Only two."

Roger pointed at Maria. "And they murdered your boyfriend."

She nodded. "And you?"

Roger shrugged and smiled. "Nobody."

"You're not married," Ten said.

"Divorced. Let them have her." He gave them a half smile, then quickly wiped it from his face. "I'm sorry. That was insensitive."

The waitress interrupted to take their order: two fish and chips and a meatloaf platter. Water all around. "I love diner food," Roger said after she left. "Only place you can find good meatloaf."

Ten had to laugh at their new accomplice. Like many geniuses, he had few social skills and just said what popped into his head. Then, if he got the wrong response, he back peddled until he felt safe. Ten recognized the pattern. He had been there much of his life as well. Until he met Amy. He looked out the window. "Looks like we're going to be able to get through our meal without interruption for once."

"Don't hold your breath," Maria said. She pointed to a pickup truck pulling in front of the diner.

"No suits," Ten said, leaning closer to the window.

"Good." Maria sounded satisfied.

After they ate, Ten paid the bill using one of the hundreds. The woman gave him an odd look when he handed it over but found enough change for him anyway. He felt bad but needed to start breaking the hundreds so he could have smaller bills when he needed them.

In the car, Ten pulled out the smart phone he'd bought to call Ben and Maria. He handed it to Maria. "Can you get us back onto the highway or take back roads to Crater Lake?"

"I can do that. Maybe we take the scenic route."

"Good for me," Ten said.

"I'm going to nap," Roger announced from the back seat. He leaned into the corner of the seat and closed his eyes. Ten felt a wash of calm come over him. He suddenly thought of them as a family out driving on a Sunday afternoon. The whole idea of ISTI, nanobots, switchable diseases, all sounded so science fiction to him. What were they doing? What had they done?

"Turn left up here," Maria said from beside him. She looked happier with something to do. Sitting and driving gave them all too much time to think. Activity would make a huge difference. "Three miles and we'll make a right."

Ten was glad that his attention could be aimed at Maria and Roger, and his driving. Whatever they had done was behind them. They had a nice meal and were on the road again. He hoped Roger really did know where Jacob Sempter would be hiding.

Chapter 22

The road kicked up a lot of dirt, so Ten slowed down. What if Jacob wasn't alone? No use in announcing themselves.

"It's up to you, from here," Maria told Roger, who had woken up as soon as the car started to jostle over the bumps in the dirt road.

"Only been here once, and never in this part of the area." Roger looked around. "It all looks the same to me. But according to what I was told, we're on the right track. Should I call my—"

"No more calls," Ten interrupted. "If you think we're on the right track…" Ten stopped the car. "What's that?" He pointed to some color off behind a few trees.

"Probably Jacob's Jeep," Roger said.

"We'll walk from here." Ten opened the door and stepped out of the car.

"You going to turn it off?" Roger asked.

"Not yet. I don't want to have to cross the wires in a hurry." Ten removed a pistol from his pack and put an extra magazine in his back pocket. "Let's prepare."

Roger appeared to be happy to have the gun in his hand again. Maria took one of the guns from Ten but didn't look very happy about it. He doubted she'd use it, but it could turn nasty, so who knew? Maybe she would. "If one bullet flies, we split up. Maria, you lay low and try to make it back to the car. Roger, go right, into the woods. And I'll go left into the woods. We can circle around on them." He narrowed his eyes at Roger. "No matter what, I have to know if Jacob is okay or not. We need his information."

"Gotcha," Roger said. He lifted his pistol so it pointed into the air and placed both hands on the grip like someone from a TV cop show ready to break into an apartment.

Ten wasn't too sure about Roger. That's the kind of person who could kill one of his own by accident. But that's all the help he had. "Let's go," he said.

Sure enough, a second car sat near the Jeep, and a small shed-like building appeared a short distance farther down the dirt road. "Not good," Ten said. He motioned for Maria to go back and for Roger to peel off into the woods. Roger nodded and stepped from the dirt road. Maria shook her head no and followed behind Roger as though she didn't trust him either. At least, that's what Ten hoped was the reason. So far, none of his team paid much attention to him, and he felt a bit unorganized because of it. Everyone needs a good plan, he thought, but they didn't have one and that was his fault.

Closer to the house, Ten heard a lot of noise inside, as though tables or desks were being overturned. The shed wasn't really that big, so he was surprised at the level of noise. He even heard glass breaking. When he approached a window, he saw two men inside who were looking for something. One looked pretty mad and was overturning everything. The other man just looked frustrated. Well, the frustrated man glanced out the window and saw Ten. He screamed, "Someone's here!" and headed for the door.

Ten didn't skip a beat; as soon as the door even began to open, he blasted it with three shots. The door stood in place for a few moments, then the frustrated man's body dropped past it, dead. The side window broke and a bullet hit Ten in the side. He fell to his knees. Then he heard Roger yelling and shooting as he rushed into the shed with his gun pulsing out bullets one by one, then everything went quiet.

Ten checked his side. This time there was a lot of blood

and it hurt like hell. His shoulder still hurt too. How many times did he have to get hit before he caught a lethal bullet?

Maria ran to him and assessed the situation. "Where are we?" she asked.

"Huh?"

"Where are we?"

"In the Oregon hills somewhere. Near Crater Lake Park." He gave her a funny look, then realized what she was determining.

"How do you feel?"

"In pain, but that's all. I don't feel terribly weak. It just hurts a lot."

Maria set her gun down beside him and ripped his shirt, pulling a good half of it from his body. "Looks worse than it is."

"Really?"

She wadded up the shirt and immediately began to compress the wound. "You are the luckiest man I've ever met."

"I don't feel lucky."

"Ripped a lot of skin off, but didn't hit anything important," she said. "How do you manage to get hit so many times, but never…"

Ten knew what she was getting at. He shook his head. He had just wondered the same thing.

Roger came out of the shed with the gun in his hand. "That guy won't be bothering us anymore."

"What about Sempter?" Ten asked.

"Not there."

"You looked everywhere?"

Roger turned around and looked inside. "There's a tiny loft for a bed, a shower-toilet area, and the rest is all one room: sink, desk, some equipment on a bench—or was on a bench, I presume—and a few chairs." Roger smiled. "And two dead guys."

"Get them out of there," Maria ordered.

"Yes, ma'am." Roger swung into action by grabbing the arms of the man lying across the threshold and dragging him out to the side of the shed.

"What are we going to do?" she asked Ten.

"Wait for Sempter. He must be out hiking or something."

"What do you think they were looking for?"

"Anything. They probably don't even know." Ten lifted her hand, which held a piece of his rolled-up shirt against his side. She let him lift the compress away to show a large area of flesh exposed. "Stitches might be nice."

Maria placed his hand over the compress and stood. "I'll check their car for a first aid kit. I doubt there are stitches, but there must be antiseptic and gauze. We can at least wrap you up. It's going to hurt for a while though."

Ten smiled and yelled after her, "I have a high pain threshold!"

Roger dragged the second man out of the shed and around to the side with the first one. "We can't let them sit out there. Bears," he said.

"Good point, but what do we do with them?"

Roger held up a finger. "I'll take care of that." He headed down the road toward the cars. Even before Maria returned with the first aid kit, Roger had driven around Jacob's Jeep and the ISTI agents' car to the side of the shed. He opened the trunk of the Camry and Ten heard him grunting as he must have been loading the dead bodies into the car.

"You doing okay?" Maria asked.

"You snuck up on me." Ten pulled his hand away. His fingers were sticky, but the blood had slowed.

"I don't want you to move yet, so stay put. I'm going into the cabin to get some water to clean this up." She set the kit on the ground next to Ten.

He shook his head. He didn't care what she did as long as it helped.

She returned with a bowl of water and a few hand towels, and proceeded to clean around the wound. "Still seeping blood, but much better. You must be protected by angels or something, because you've gotten in the way too often to not be dead."

"Thanks for that," Ten said.

"I mean it. I suppose it sounds bad, but it's really a good thing so far."

"So far?"

She just smiled at him.

After Roger loaded the trunk of the Camry, he drove away, down the dirt road again. Ten couldn't see how far Roger went from where he lay on the ground, so he let it go. Roger could do whatever he liked with the bodies, Ten didn't care.

In a few minutes, Roger jogged into view. He looked tired, probably out of shape. He bypassed Maria and Ten and went straight into the shed.

"You think ISTI will send more men?" she asked.

"At this point, I'm not sure what the hell to think. We don't know if these people were acting on behalf of ISTI or some other group wanting our technology. You can't trust anyone." He cringed, then closed his eyes. "Except maybe each other."

"Unless one of us would consider selling the technology."

"Only the technology we know, but, yeah, except for that," Ten said.

"If we share as much of our knowledge as you'd like, we'll all have enough information to make a lot of money." She hesitated. "You think we can each keep that secret?"

"This is dangerous stuff."

"Some people don't care."

"You suggesting Sempter? Or Roger?"

"No, not at all. I just want to be realistic. Anyone could turn everyone else in. The more of us there are, the more money we're worth."

"I don't want to think about it," he said.

CHAPTER 23

Roger had done a fair job of cleaning up by the time Maria wrapped Ten's wound and helped him into the shed-sized cabin. The bench sat upright, and a lot of equipment had been replaced and organized. There was a portable oscilloscope, a multimeter, a simulator of some kind, and several printed circuit boards and parts. "What do you think he's been up to?" Ten wondered out loud.

"Maybe he's no dummy either and was trying to figure out a way to undo this whole mess," Roger said.

"Maybe."

"How long do we wait here?" Maria wanted to know. "I get nervous when we're too still."

"Me too." Ten took a breath and winced. "I hate to say this, but maybe we should hide in the woods and just watch the place until we make a decision, come up with a plan."

"We should get the guns, then." Roger got up from a chair and walked toward the door. "Probably should have all our stuff either way. If anyone found our car, we'd be screwed. They'd kill us with our own weapons."

"Good idea," Ten said. After Roger left, he started to get up.

"Where you going?" Maria quickly stepped toward him to help.

"I'm not moving very quickly. Maybe I should get out of here first. At least you two can run if you have to."

"We're not running anywhere as long as you're alive and with us. We can hide if you want, but we're not leaving you for any reason. Besides, we still haven't transferred any important information to one another. That's next. There must be some real basic knowledge that would lead any one of us into understanding what we need to rebuild any and all of the parts."

"That's the hope. Because if we can build it, we are that much closer to destroying it."

"It's a doomsday disease enabler if we can't stop this. Worse than any chemical warfare we could possibly come up with. I don't like it." She stopped talking and started to help Ten to his feet.

"I don't like it either. But I also have confidence we can figure this out. We can shut this project down one way or another."

"And start getting laws implemented to protect the general population against injection of such a potentially dangerous nanobiotic disease enabler," she said.

"Let's go." Ten placed his arm around Maria's shoulder and walked gingerly out the door and down the two steps to the ground. He glanced around for a path. "Maybe in the back." As they walked around the building, they heard footsteps, then saw a tall, lanky man with a walking stick and backpack. They stopped.

"Who are you? And what's going on?"

"Sempter?"

"Don't know who you're talking about," the man said. "I'm just a hiker."

Ten held out his hand. "Tempest Nesbit."

"Maria Tanner."

The man looked from one to the other. "Who else is here?"

"Roger Floramo," Maria said.

The man smiled. "Well, who is on their way then? You must have been followed."

"There were already two men ransacking your place," Ten said. "They got here before we did."

"What the hell…" Jacob Sempter walked toward them.

Ten held up his hand. "We took care of them. Don't worry. But we can't stay here."

Jacob looked past them. "You must be Roger."

Ten turned and saw that Roger held onto his backpack and the munitions bag along with two other bags. They must have weighed a ton. He let them drop. "Guilty as charged," Roger said.

Jacob walked past Ten and Maria and shook Roger's hand. "Nice design you have there. If we could create larger ones… holy shit!"

"Thank you." They shook vigorously.

"Bink said you were a genius."

"He's no slouch either," Roger said.

Jacob shook his head. "That's why I knew it must be true."

"So, how'd you find out about my design?" Roger asked.

Jacob laughed loudly and turned around to look at Ten and Maria. "The people who try to keep things from us are about as smart as a lab rat, that's how. I started to put two and two together pretty quickly. You don't get to work on a top secret project on your own and yet that's exactly what they had me doing. So I did my own research. I didn't know for sure that you were involved until I saw you. But I do know about your work, partly from Bink." He swung around and pointed at Ten. "Code sequencing, right?"

Ten cocked his head. The man was smart.

"And Dr. Tanner. You've worked with every major pharm company in the country in one manner or other. I've seen your photo all over the place. You must be involved with integration or delivery?"

"Integration," Maria said. "Delivery is Gary Satterfield."

"He's with Zephyr Biomed, isn't he?" She nodded. "Where you headed?" Jacob walked closer to Ten and Maria.

"To hide somewhere," Ten said. "We can't stay here. We don't know how many more might be showing up now that these two won't be answering their calls."

"Do you know who they are?"

"We do. They're called ISTI."

"International Security for Technological Innovations. I've heard of them." Jacob reached toward Ten. "You shot?"

"Yeah. And I'm getting tired. Can we go somewhere I can rest?"

"Sure. I'll just leave my stuff in the cabin for now. They won't know what the hell it is anyway." He walked past them, back the way he'd come. "Follow me."

Ten and Maria took some of the packs from Roger. Ten didn't move very quickly and soon had to sit and rest. "Leave me for now. You guys go on and I'll follow behind. As long as you're on the hikers' path, I should be fine."

"Not going to happen," Roger said.

"We're in this together." Maria checked his bandage. "You're not bleeding, just sore."

"I'd say a little more than sore," Ten said.

Jacob stopped up ahead and turned around, then walked quickly back toward them. "I'll handle him from here. You two walk ahead of me. I'll guide you." He slid an arm under Ten's arm and lifted him with ease. "You're pretty solid," he said.

"I work out," Ten said.

"Good for you." Jacob pointed for the others to walk ahead. "Go. Go."

Maria and Roger hopped to it. About a half mile up the path—they were making much better time—Jacob told them to dart to the left. "Between those two big cedars. There won't be a path anymore, so keep an eye on that spot of light coming through in front of you. The mountain opens to a stream about there." Within the thick canopy of trees, Ten saw the opening Jacob pointed out. It looked as though several trees had fallen and left a hole in the woods for the sky to shine through. But before they made it, Jacob had them shoot off to the left again, as though heading back toward the cabin. "Another thirty, forty yards you'll see my lean-to. That'll keep us out of the rain."

"How often are you up here?" Ten asked.

"Not often enough." When they reached the lean-to, Jacob lowered Ten onto the ground. "So, I take it you're the leader? What's the plan?"

"Knowledge exchange," Roger said as he situated the things he carried. "That way no matter who gets killed, we can stop this thing from occurring."

Jacob laughed. "You really think you can stop it permanently?"

"No," Ten said. "All we have to do is stop it once and we've sent the message."

"You know they'll come after us all," Jacob said. He leaned against the side of his lean-to. Maria and Roger sat under it, but toward the opening.

"They're already after us. They've already done a lot of damage."

"How is it you guys are still alive?" Jacob asked.

Ten shrugged. The question made him wonder why Jacob was alive. "A number of reasons. Some of our bodyguards were not killers, some were wanting to sell what we know. Look, we know this is crazy, but it's either continue forward or let them capture us. Then, it could be they kill us outright or they sell us to some foreign country, who knows?"

"None of those options sound good to me," Roger said.

Maria started to cry and put her hand over her eyes. Jacob reached toward her, but she waved him away. "I'm okay."

"I just wanted to do my work." Jacob looked around and stopped at Ten. "So?"

"How'd you make it without getting killed?" The question was direct, but Jacob made no indication that it bothered him.

"I saw it coming." He lowered his gaze. "Truth is, what you're calling bodyguards, I called a pain in the ass. This guy always hanging around me. I couldn't wait to get away from him." He waved his arms around as though including their surroundings. "This is more me. I don't like people much. I'd rather be out here or in my lab." He blinked a few times, then turned away. "Lucky."

"How so?" Ted asked.

"I saw the guy heading for my front door. I was upstairs working on my own project. His jacket opened and I saw the gun. Took off out the back door."

"He had no idea where you'd go?"

"He didn't know me for shit," Jacob said.

Ten felt satisfied and nodded to the others. "We've figured a lot of this out already. We know what they're up to. Now we have to figure out how to stop them."

"Transfer of knowledge," Roger said again. "Mine is fairly simple." Everyone laughed when he said that, even Maria. "What?"

Ten said, "You've got some of the brightest talent in the US sitting here. Trust me; none of this is that simple."

Roger chuckled then went into an explanation of how his nanobots restructured themselves to fit into multiple different protocols, how they could mimic certain molecules and appear like something they're not. But their programming takes "a bit of vigorous code crunching. A combination of what I call gyros and magnetics. It's not really that, but very similar."

"We may get to that later." Ten turned toward Jacob. "And you?"

Jacob admitted to designing a Wi-Fi code delivery system that could easily control the nanobots from a central location. "Multiple signals can be created and delivered through already-present cell towers." He closed his eyes. "With my equipment, anyone who has access could start a pandemic, dial in how fast it spreads and to whom, then flick a switch, figuratively, and kill hundreds of thousands of people."

He opened his eyes. "What were we thinking?"

Chapter 24

The evening wore on. Jacob had some food and so did Ten and the others. They'd make it that far. But now what? Maria suggested they not try to figure too much out until they'd slept on it. "We're all tired and overwhelmed at the moment."

"I have a blanket and a sleeping bag," Jacob said. "I don't need anything."

"Me either," Roger said. "Let's keep Ten warm enough to fight off any infection."

Maria took the sleeping bag Jacob held toward her. "Don't do this because I'm a woman."

"Too late," Jacob said. "We might be geeks, but we're chivalrous geeks. Can't fault us for that." After everyone found a place to sleep and got settled, Jacob packed all their food into one bag and wandered away from the lean-to to where he had a rope draped over a tall branch. He attached the bag, hoisted it into the air, and secured the rope to the tree trunk.

Roger handed each of them a gun. "In case."

"You won't have to worry up here," Jacob promised. He looked nervous about all the weapons. "But if that's what you want…"

"I'll feel better," Roger said.

Ten wasn't sure anyone else would feel safe with Roger holding a gun in his sleep, but he let it slide. He wished they could build a fire but knew that would be stupid. He tried to get as comfortable as possible, even though his side pulsed and he felt terribly uncomfortable no matter how he positioned himself. Eventually he dropped off to sleep.

When Ten awoke the next morning, Jacob was gone, which brought him fully awake as soon as he realized it was only the three of them again. Pain shot through his side when he tried to sit up. He moved slowly and secured every move with an arm for support. Each shift into a more upright position came with a shot of pain.

Maria stirred and woke up next. She popped her head out of the sleeping bag, then slid her body out. "I have to pee." She rushed behind the lean-to and Ten heard her wandering farther away. In a few minutes, she came back and knelt by his side. "I feel filthy," she said. Her hair hung in a tangled mess and her breath smelled stale. She swung around to Roger's organized area of packs and bags and retrieved the first aid kit she'd stolen from the ISTI car. "Let's change this wrap, shall we?"

"Sure." Ten had to pee too, but could hold it until she finished. He wanted to see how things were progressing anyway. He did reach for his shoulder; it felt itchy more than anything. "Goodness, I have more near hits."

"Angels, I already told you that." She pulled the bandage from his side and inspected his wound. "Doesn't look too bad under the circumstances." She set the bloodied wrap on the ground and began preparing another bandage for his side.

"I wish we had something to stitch this together."

"We'll do with what we have." She affixed the bandage to his side. "So where do you think Jacob went early this morning?"

"You thinking he's bringing them to us?" Ten asked.

"Checking on his equipment," Roger said sleepily. "That's what I'd do."

"And if they're watching? If others came by?" Maria said. "Not too bright. He could have us all in danger."

"Should we move?" Roger asked. He stretched his arms and legs and yawned.

"We'll wait a little while," Ten said. "Anyone know when he left?" He looked at each of the others. Nothing. "Roger, could you get the food down? We'll have something quick and then make a decision."

"Deal." Roger got up and wandered toward their food, hanging from the tree.

Ten reached for Maria. "Help me up. I've got to use the men's room." He leaned on her and she lifted him. Standing was easier than he'd thought. Walking didn't seem so bad at the moment either, but that might be because his focus was on having to pee. Didn't matter. He walked to the rear of the lean-to, then out behind a tree, and relieved himself. When he got back, Roger had a banana, an apple, and an energy bar sitting near where Ten's pistol lay on the ground.

Roger pointed. "Breakfast is served."

They chatted about what they'd learned from one another. "You guys can figure this out," she said.

"Us?" Roger laughed.

"I'm an integrator," she said in response. "I make sure the switches and the bots interconnect the way they're supposed to. You two know the inter-workings better than I do."

"What if they didn't integrate?" Roger asked.

Ten cocked his head. "Sure. If all the pieces are there, but they don't integrate, then what? Nothing, right?"

"That was the easiest part of my job. Trust me, anyone can do that, and once they're integrated, nothing can tear them apart." She gave them a big, fake smile. "Sorry, boys."

"What happens when you need to adjust what the nanobots do?" Ten asked Roger.

"Easy. You send a reconfiguration signal for the new format. There are thirty-two segments, each with eight sides. There are diseases we haven't even discovered yet that we can cure just through a reconfiguration process." Roger looked proud of himself.

"But to reconfigure, they have to—"

"Release," Maria and Roger said simultaneously.

Roger shook his head.

"Why not?" Ten asked.

"It's all one code. My design doesn't take a release code without also having a reconfigure code. Failsafe. I didn't want them falling apart in there just because of a glitch in the new format construction."

Ten snapped his fingers. "There must be a stable, non-threatening format you can put them into. Like a holding pattern?"

"Maybe, but they'd still be there. Someone could figure out your sequencing codes, or Jacob's Wi-Fi signals." Roger didn't look as though he was buying it.

"Vitamins?" Maria said. "If you can make them appear as a vitamin, they could pass through the kidney. I know that sounds crazy."

Roger's face lit up. "You know…" He glanced to the side as though thinking.

"Then they're out of the system completely," Maria said.

Ten shook his head back and forth. "Brilliant."

"Indeed," came Jacob's voice from twenty feet away. Everyone turned and looked at him. He smiled from ear to ear. "You've got a great idea there." He walked closer and knelt next to Roger, reached out, and snatched his pistol from the ground. He pointed it at them. "Too bad you won't get to use this information." He turned his head. "Come on, guys!" he yelled.

Three men stepped from behind trees and came closer.

"We've been hiding here for an hour waiting for you sleepyheads to wake up." Jacob reached for Ten's gun, and Maria's, both lying on the ground near where they had slept.

"You sold us out," Ten said.

"No. I had most of this figured out anyway. These guys are buyers."

"From where?"

"Doesn't matter. I don't care." Jacob stood up. "I get to do all the research I want, with all the money I need, and they'll pay for it—for the rest of my life." He looked proud of himself. "They're all yours," he said. "But don't hurt them yet. We might need a little bit more information first."

The men came over and lifted Ten a bit rougher than he would have liked. Roger and Maria went without rebuttal. As Ten passed Jacob, the lanky man said, "Game."

Ten almost felt relieved. No more questions as to when they'd get caught. They could do nothing now. They'd lost.

Checkmate

CHAPTER 25

A real laboratory. A locked room. And rougher than necessary handlers. To Ten, it appeared as though Jacob Sempter was in charge, even though everyone knew—hopefully, even Sempter—that once these people understood the process well enough, it would be all over for them. They'd all be killed.

"Handlers" were what Jacob called the men who leaned over Ten's shoulder as he worked for the first few days, making sure he didn't try anything—like that was an option. They had been transported blindfolded in the back of a van, but only drove for about an hour and a half. They were still in Oregon.

It had been almost two weeks since they'd arrived. It had taken that long to get things set up in the lab, even after Jacob's equipment was installed. Without knowing what each of them had worked on specifically, or what equipment they needed, the criminals had to go on a buying spree.

The lab looked as though it belonged in a doctor's clinic for the most part. Blinds were closed all the time. The rooms they stayed in were windowless, internal to the building, probably exam rooms. During that first week, a professional who didn't speak English, or pretended not to, stitched Ten's side and cared for him. The handlers almost never spoke and when they did it was in low tones, difficult to tell what language it was, but it was Spanish based for sure. Drug cartel? Ten had no idea and cared less as time went on.

"Morning," Roger greeted Ten as he entered the small kitchen area near the lab.

"Sleep well?" Ten selected an egg sandwich from the freezer and microwaved it.

"Yeah," Roger said. "You feeling better again today?"

"I am." He rubbed his side. "Not perfect. I'm starting to need some exercise too. Being cooped up isn't good for me."

Maria walked into the kitchen, said good morning, and reached for the freezer door. She, too, selected an egg sandwich. She held it up, "Protein."

"Where are the handlers this morning?" Ten asked. "I heard someone unlock my door, and by the time I got dressed, no one stood outside waiting for me as usual."

"Maybe they figured we're not going anywhere," Roger said.

Maria scoffed. "Maybe they're waiting for us to try to escape so they have a reason to shoot us."

"Don't think about it," Ten said. "We've got everything we need here to try all our theories out. Let's focus on that."

"But we're communicating directly now." Roger didn't look happy. "They'll know exactly what we're doing. They won't need us for much longer. And you know our government has already started applying this dial-in death stuff we're working on. So even if they're still looking for us, it's to kill us. Where would we escape to?" He looked exhausted just talking about it. "What's the use?"

"So? Who cares what our government's doing? Or what these people plan to do? Our job is in front of us." Ten tried to be cryptic.

"When we figure out how to disengage the bots, they won't like it." Roger's eyes grew wide. He had lost a few pounds and his pants didn't appear to fit properly. Nerves.

Ten pulled his sandwich from the microwave and found a place at the table. "They're probably listening to our conversation. You know that, don't you?"

"Should we be more careful?" Roger asked through a mouthful of a second bagel with cream cheese.

"Maybe," Maria said. "But it's too late now, isn't it? Maybe from this point forward? At the moment, Jacob could probably do most of this himself."

Ten shook his head. "Not likely. He's a hardware guy. He needs to be working with components large enough to see."

"You're a hardware guy," she countered.

"Micro hardware," Ten said. "Jacob's more of a macro hardware guy."

"He could oversee someone else, then. He knows how this is supposed to work."

"Still not likely. He's probably not used to looking at this stuff the way we are. He's developing a large hardware and software switching center, essentially. Our sequencing programs and processes aren't that easily transferable if you haven't worked with them for a long time," Ten explained. "At least that's how I see it. I could be wrong. Maybe they're just using us because we're handy. Why hire someone else when the monkeys you have are working fine."

A handler stepped into the kitchen and jerked his head, indicating they should get to work.

"This is a unique situation," Ten said. "We get to work everything out."

"Then they take it." Maria was just taking her sandwich from the microwave. It steamed in her hand. She took a tentative bite. "Can I finish this?"

Ten walked over and put one arm around her, while the other held the last of his sandwich. He leaned in close. "We escape soon," he mumbled into her ear. They all knew they were getting close to a solution to disengaging the nanobots, and Ten felt their lives were getting more tenuous every day.

"Yeah, it is a good sandwich," she replied.

Midmorning, Jacob came into the room. It was late for him. He had his own equipment in a corner of the lab but didn't do much other than piddle with it. Jacob was ready for testing, even if the rest of them weren't. He walked over to them, standing in close proximity at two lab tables pushed together. "We've got to test this soon," he said to Ten. Then he leaned in closely. "I'm sorry."

"So am I."

Jacob shoved Ten aside and tapped on the table. "This could get messy."

Ten sensed that Jacob wasn't being clear on purpose. "What's going on?"

"Only three handlers in the building. It's D-Day," he whispered. Jacob pulled back for a moment, rearranged a few things on the bench, then bent to look into a microscope.

"You're helping us escape?" Ten asked. Then he saw Maria out the corner of his eye as she stepped closer to them.

"Everything okay over here?" she asked.

"Yeah, yeah. I'll be with you in a minute. I think I figured something out." Ten turned back to his bench and Jacob. "What the hell's going on?"

"You needed a lab. They caught me red-handed." He laughed out loud as though Ten had told him a joke. "Told you they were idiots."

Ten couldn't help but laugh too.

"Test run this afternoon." Jacob left Ten at the bench and walked over to his own area. One of the handlers walked over to him and said something in English. Ten recognized the inflections.

Jacob talked with him for a moment and the man gave a short laugh, then shrugged.

"You have to be a scientist to get it," he said loud enough for everyone to hear.

Ten, Maria, and Roger conferred about testing. They wanted to try several tests before the big one that afternoon.

Ten informed Roger and Maria about Jacob, which helped. They needed his equipment to test their deconstruct process. This would make things easier in the long run. They'd have all the information they needed.

"Preliminary testing would help," he said to Jacob, while standing next to him. "Then, this afternoon we can pull off the primary test. Will we have visitors?"

"Probably, if we're still here," Jacob said.

"That soon?"

"Others arrive around four." He tapped the table. "And that's why it's D-Day."

One of the handlers walked over to Jacob and said something in Spanish that Ten didn't recognize. Jacob responded, then looked at Ten. "They don't like us talking so much," he said to Ten. "First test is one hour from now. Then lunch." He looked at the handler and repeated what he'd said in Spanish. At least that's what Ten assumed.

The man said, "Okay."

Ten noticed what looked like a Glock sticking from the man's belt and suspected all three stashed their weapons in the same place. He wasn't looking for weapons until now. So how do four geeky scientists escape three armed captors? He made his way to where Maria worked—actually, not doing much at this point—and told her about the timing and about the guns.

"Get them together," she said. "Close proximity to the four of us and we have the best shot… no pun intended. Either that or separate them, but that's not likely. There's always two of them in the room at a time. Maybe we take those two first." She shrugged. "You tell me." She got back to her busywork and Ten went back to his work.

In a few more minutes, he called Roger over and explained that they were going to try to get the three handlers closer together, then attack—he figured Maria's first idea was the best—but not until around two o'clock.

"In the meantime, we're going to test this thing out in fifteen minutes."

"I hope it works the way we want it to," Roger said.

Ten smiled at him. "It has to look as though it failed the first time or two."

The handlers combed the room, walking around whenever they got tired of just standing at the doorways—there were two, one on either end of the lab. One of the handlers stood near Maria. Ten watched as she moved a few items around on her bench and knocked over two small containers. What looked like steam poured into the air. She jumped back. "Acid!" she yelled.

The handler jumped back too. "Acid, acid," he said.

Maria grabbed a rag and started to wipe it up, while Ten grabbed a towel and rushed over to help. The handler remained close to them, close enough for Ten to snatch his gun, but he didn't do that. Instead, he said, "Please step out of the way," and pushed into the handler slightly. The man felt solid.

He backed up a few steps. "Why acid?" he asked. So they spoke a little English.

Maria looked him in the eye. "In case something goes wrong. It's a fast kill."

He appeared to buy it, even though Ten knew there was no acid. She had dumped a few crystals of dry ice on her bench and spilled water on it. He could feel the cold through the towel. He could only guess what she was up to.

Chapter 26

The first trial didn't work very well, but they did a second one twenty minutes later and every nanobot disengaged. Roger gave a sour look and shook his head as though the experiment didn't work again. They all said, "Ohhhhh," as though they were disappointed for yet another failure. The guards didn't look like they cared either way, like they hardly knew what it all meant. It wasn't their problem.

Ten cornered Jacob and asked the big question, "Is there any way to build a skeleton key that would unlock all of them, no matter what code I give them?"

"Not that I know of," Jacob said. "I'll give it some thought though."

"We'd have to go through all kinds of number string combinations to get rid of this all at once. Millions of combinations. There must be a way."

Roger wandered over and looked at the two of them. "That's only one," he said.

"We were just saying that," Ten said. "Now what? We could spend the rest of our lives running through the numbers. The technology was created to address one person at a time. Maybe the government—" He paused and turned to glance at the goons "—or these guys, have the equipment to run through the codes, but we don't."

"Then we failed, even if we won," Roger said.

"Not yet," Jacob said. "Let's pull the trigger one more time and go to lunch."

"Fine with me," Ten said. They could probably fit in one or two more runs before two o'clock, then they were through. When they broke for lunch, he said, "It's been nice having a lab to work in. I must say that."

"Enough people have died," Maria said while staring into the corner of the room. Her microwaved lunch of some kind of casserole sat in front of her, hardly eaten.

"I know," Ten said.

"I know you know," Maria swung around and looked right at him, "but they don't. Neither of them had loved ones who've died. Maybe this doesn't seem as urgent to them?"

"Hold on now," Roger said. "I'm taking this seriously."

Jacob just got up and left. "I have to think," he said as he walked from the lunchroom.

Maria leaned forward. "It's not just to be taken seriously. It's more than that. It's life or death. Not of one person, but potentially millions. You can't know the magnitude of that where you're sitting. You have little connection to it."

Roger tightened his lips and shook his head at her as though he had no words to respond with. He jerked his chair backward as he stood, toppling it over. A guard ran to the door, his gun pulled. When he saw Roger picking the chair back up, he turned and left. Roger reached and grabbed the dessert brownie from his own meal and walked out of the room behind the guard.

Ten reached out to take Maria's hand.

"I miss him," she said.

"I know. I miss Amy. I miss my life before all this started. And I miss who I was." He scrunched up his face and narrowed his eyes at her. "I'm okay with killing these goons and they probably have families too. What's happened in a few weeks?"

"I don't know. But this is more important than either of us." She glanced at the door Roger, Jacob, and the guard had left through. "More important than all of us."

"But even if what we do works, we'd have to run through all the codes. Or we'd have to get our hands on some pretty amazing equipment to do it."

"Why?"

"That's right. You weren't there. Our trial only killed one nanobot string. The one we all coded properly and integrated."

"Yeah, but it wiped out the gyro or magnetics or something, right? Isn't that what Roger said?"

"Yeah, but we need the whole string to do that."

Maria shook her head. "No, you don't."

Ten leaned in to explain. "Roger said—"

"That disengage command was part of the string. That it couldn't create a reconnect without telling the nanobot what to do first, then the reconnect signal. There's some kind of feedback to do that."

"Yeah. That's right but—"

She interrupted him again. "Run a fake string," she said quietly, looking directly at him. "The nanobot will recognize the deconstruct, then feedback will tell it there's more information in the string, even though there's no actual code for a proper reconstruct."

"Won't it kick it out?"

"Why? If the reconnect is just looking to make sure the space is filled and it's not some kind of glitch?"

Ten jumped from his seat and rushed out to where Roger sat with his hands over his eyes. When Ten tapped him on the shoulder, Roger lowered his hands and turned his head slowly toward Ten. His eyes were red. "I understand. I have loved ones. This matters to me. I don't want anyone to die."

"I know, man. She was just feeling sorry for herself. We both are. I'm sorry she took it out on you. That wasn't right. But you can handle it."

"She had no right," he said.

"I know. I know. But I have to ask you a question."

"What?"

Ten asked about the sequencing codes.

Roger glanced away, then back, then away. "Normally, it has to see some kind of configuration. The magnetic reattachment code has to be in there or it won't disengage in the first place."

"That's what I thought." Ten started to turn away.

"Except that… that might work if I offer it something it can't do, or something that renders it useless."

"One code fits all?" Ten asked.

Roger got a big smile across his face.

"You create that code, I'll format it for the switches, and Maria can integrate it. We'll create several different nanobot configurations and see if it clears them all," Ten said. "Everything that's out there looks exactly like what we're doing, only we're creating it from scratch each time."

Roger wiped his eyes with the back of his hands and sniffed. "We'll have them ball up. They'll be useless that way."

"But they can get a different code and be transformed again, can't they?"

Roger shook his head. "Not if I told them to lock that way."

"You can do that?"

Roger smiled. "I can do that."

"I'll inform the others," Ten said.

Ten rushed toward the lunchroom to tell Maria first. She had a forlorn look on her face, like she had been abandoned. He sat next to her and whispered their plan.

She smiled. "Good," she said. "Now that's better." But she didn't look as though it was better. She looked tired and a little resigned to the situation, even though things were looking up.

Maybe she considered their escape and worried about that. He couldn't think about it. It was her problem at the moment. There was work to be done. Nonetheless, Ten took her hand in his. "We can do this."

"What if they have people outside too? Wouldn't that be logical?"

"For us, perhaps. But if what Jacob believes is true, they're all idiots. They're bigger than we are. They have weapons. And we're just a bunch of geeky scientists. They could have their guard down."

"Could."

"I'm going to go with *do* have their guard down," he said.

When Maria walked to her bench, Ten and Roger were already at work. Ten noticed the guards had rotated through and suspected they took turns eating their lunches. They never sat with their captors. Their conduct had become relaxed as they saw that the scientists weren't going anywhere either. Ten figured it made them more vulnerable.

One of the guards came over and grabbed Jacob and walked him from the room. Jacob came back a few minutes later by himself and walked straight over to Ten. "Wow," he said. "You won't believe what I found out."

"What? What's wrong?"

"These guys are just stiffs. They're selling our technology to the highest bidder. That's who's coming this afternoon. They don't even know what we're doing."

"How'd you find this out?"

He jerked a thumb toward the inside door he'd gone through. "The other dummy. He asked what we whispered about in the lunchroom this morning. Asked what we meant by disengage. It bothered him. He doesn't know much English but knew disengage. He said it didn't sound right. I explained that we have to disengage the nanobot before we can reconfigure it into something more dangerous."

"That's true."

"Yeah." He laughed. "That's why it was so easy to say it."

"So, four o'clock," Ten said.

"We have an hour before we get out of here."

"Sticking with two o'clock for the escape?"

"You betcha." Jacob walked back to his bench.

Roger delivered his code information to Jacob, and Ten explained how the switches worked when they received the code sequence. Understanding that combination was essential for Jacob to create the skeleton key.

"I'll be ready in less than ten minutes," Jacob said to the two of them. "And with this information, I can download the answer to a thumb drive. All I'll need is some higher power cell equipment and we can stop these things."

"That's our next battle," Ten said.

It took longer than ten minutes for everything to be in place, but once the simulation was in play, they each sat around and waited. Ten saw the smiles on everyone's faces when it worked. Knowing their handlers had no idea what they'd done, it didn't matter any longer whether they looked happy or sad about their work. And perhaps looking happy would make the handlers more at ease that things were on track. After all, they had a four o'clock meeting with a very important group of buyers. Was there one or more? Ten wondered. It hardly mattered. They'd be long gone by the time four o'clock hit.

Chapter 27

As two o'clock approached, Roger began to fidget, Maria appeared ready for anything, and Jacob sat piddling with his equipment. The sun blazed through and around the blinds. Ten hadn't seen the outside and didn't have a clue as to where they were. A clinic would be somewhere there were other buildings, although it could be located in an abandoned area. He hadn't heard any cars coming and going, not that he recalled. He glanced at the clock for about the hundredth time in a minute or two. Had it stopped? He knew better. He also knew that his nervousness might transfer to the two goons in the room. He wouldn't want that.

About three minutes before two, Jacob got up from his bench and wandered over to where the other three were situated nearer one another. He reached out with both hands and rotated his hands to call them all together. "We need to have a serious talk," he said. As soon as they were in a tight group, he whispered, "Get ready." Then he backed away. "Uh, oh." He brought his hands up as though he were surrendering. "No you don't. They'll kill you." He had only taken a few steps back. Ten was impressed by his acting ability.

The two goons rushed over to see what was going on. One said something in Spanish, while the other one reached for Jacob, saying, "What? What?"

Maria pickup up a glass and threw it in the man's face, yelling, "Acid!"

The man clawed at his eyes and raised his head while backing up. Roger shoved him at the same time that Ten reached in and yanked the gun from his belt. He swung the gun around and at close range in the chest, blasted the second goon, who reached for his gun a little too late. Roger dropped to the floor and pulled the gun from the wounded guard and pointed it at the guard he'd shoved to the ground. "Don't think about it," he said.

They all heard the third guard running down the hall toward them, and split up—except for Roger, who didn't move from where he sat.

The other guard rounded the corner into the room and shot at Roger.

Ten stood across the room and fired, but missed, then fired three more times, correcting his aim each time until the man dropped.

Jacob rushed to the last guard to check on his status while Maria rushed over to Roger, who looked woozy. "He's shot!" she yelled.

"See, I could be the next one dead," Roger said. Ten wondered why he held onto her words for so long and figured it was probably some childhood problem that, at the moment, was none of his business. Maria didn't even offer a reply.

"He's dead," Jacob said from the side of the third man. "You got him twice."

Ten felt some sort of strange satisfaction over his shooting abilities, although he also knew he shouldn't feel that way. What happens when you know what you should feel, yet that's not how you feel? he wondered. Was he becoming a killer merely by having to kill? He shook his head. Too philosophical for the moment.

"Check the other guy," Ten said. He didn't want to have to see his handy work at the moment.

Jacob had a hand on the man's neck. "Alive, but probably not for long. He has a chest wound. You know how to aim for the vulnerables," Jacob said.

"I wish it were about aiming," Ten said. "I'd aim to keep them alive."

Maria took the gun from Roger's fingers and helped him to lie back on the floor. "Get me something to clean this wound with," Maria said. She pointed at the other man. "And someone keep an eye on him."

Ten stepped up and took over for Roger and Maria. He motioned for the man to stand. The front of his clothes were wet. "What'd you splash onto him?"

"Water. I didn't want to hurt anyone," she said.

Ten heard her loud and clear, which only added to his concern he was becoming more like them with every additional kill. It didn't sit well, but it was true. What could he do about it? What did he even want to do about it? Ten tied the guard up. He glanced at the clock. It was two thirty already. Now time works like it's supposed to, he thought. "We'd better get whatever we need and get out of here."

Jacob pulled a thumb drive from his pocket. "Everything we need," he said, holding it up.

"Can he make it?" Ten asked about Roger. He feared he may have sounded crass in asking it so straightforward, but it was all he had at the moment.

"I can make it," Roger said.

"Maria's getting pretty good with wounds," Ten said.

"Only a scratch," Maria said. "He's as lucky as you."

"That's the good news." Ten glanced toward Jacob.

Jacob headed toward the door. "We're out of here."

The four of them walked down the hall to the reception area. Dust covered the countertop in the reception area and the chairs looked well used and ratty. Other than that, things looked as though they were in place, as though the business had vacated overnight. Pictures still hung on the walls. Magazines lay on tables. There were even files on some of the shelves, but not all of them. Ten wondered briefly what the story was with the place, but quickly forgot about it and moved on. The front door was bolted, so he shot the lock loose. "Go, go, go," Ten said as he held the door for them.

The sun blazed. It was so nice to be outside. He looked around and saw that they were indeed in an abandoned strip mall. The road out front was broken and grass grew from some of the cracks. That old. He had no idea at all which way they could go to get near any civilization. Mountains stood in the distance. Where the hell were they?

The other stores in the strip all appeared to be professional locations: a dental office, real estate office, and lawyer's office. He shook his head in wonderment, then regrouped and suggested they head north. Who knew where any direction led them? "We'll go off road," he said. "Through the woods so we don't accidently run into the people coming for the technology."

"Won't they be able to replicate what we've done, since our equipment and everything is still back there?" Roger asked.

"Doesn't matter anymore," Ten said. "We have the cure. Not our government and not another government can use the technology, at least not how it is right now."

Jacob relieved Maria of Roger and helped him walk. "If they're smart, our government will recognize that they need us now. We can save lives with what we know."

"Wasn't that the idea in the first place?" Maria said.

Ten led them across the road and down the street toward the end of the strip mall. "I'm afraid none of us knows what the idea was in the first place. We assumed it was to save lives. Maybe that's what they wanted us to assume if we ever got close to understanding what we were doing, but we don't know. We'll probably never know."

"There's enough information back there to allow any group of intelligent people to figure out what we were up to. It's pretty much out of the bag whether we like it or not," Jacob said.

"But we got out alive," Roger said.

"That is a bonus," Ten said.

"For now." Maria didn't sound too happy with their potential future or their escape. She almost sounded disappointed. She caught up with Ten as they bent down and ran for a patch of bushes. "Someone's coming!" she yelled.

Jacob and Roger were right behind Ten and Maria. Roger grunted when Jacob dropped him to the ground. "Get over it. We don't need to get caught a second time."

Jacob started to lean toward an opening in the brush and Roger grabbed his arm. "Wait until they drive by, they're less likely to see you peeking around the bushes at them."

Jacob waited. "Looks ominous," he said, "and they're pulling up to the building."

Ten looked behind them. "Let's go. It'll take them a few minutes to figure out what happened and decide whether to collect our equipment or call in the specialists." He saw what looked like an abandoned playground off the street behind them. "We'll head that way." He got up, waved for them to follow, and began to jog toward the playground in the hopes that somewhere nearby there would be trees or something they could hide in for a while. He glanced behind him and Maria was on his tail. Jacob and Roger were coming after her, although slower. He turned back. He had no plan but getting as far from that clinic as possible was a good beginning.

Chapter 28

As evening settled in, the four of them huddled down. They were well protected somewhere in the middle of a wooded area. They had not eaten since lunch, but no one complained. Ten and Jacob held onto the two pistols, one magazine full and the other with eleven rounds. Maria complained that she didn't want to go on any longer. "I've had enough."

"We all have," Jacob said. "But what choice have we got?"

"Turn ourselves in," Ten said.

Everyone laughed.

"I mean it," he said.

"I don't care if they shoot me," Maria said. "At least then it'd be over."

Ten knew she vacillated back and forth between wanting to go on and wishing she were done with it all, even if she were dead. He had no idea how she could go back and forth with such extremes. He reached for her and shook his head. "Our government needs us. But more importantly, the rest of the world, all those other people, need what we know to keep them safe. We can't let any government have something like this. We just can't."

"The government—ours or someone else's—will just abuse the science. That's what happens. They always do," Roger said. "Don't you think it's unreasonable to assume they won't do the same with this?"

"Yeah. I agree with Roger." Jacob sat with his legs crossed and his head against a tree trunk. "What do we do about that?"

Ten thought about it. "We broadcast it. We write papers. Yes, people can try to create a way to block our attempts, but there are always hackers. Get enough people on any one subject and you've got no way to keep it all to yourself."

"If we're alive, we can broadcast it," Jacob said.

"You called them idiots," Ten said. "We should be able to negotiate with them, our own government for sure. Now that they've been after us, don't you think they're wondering who else has the technology?"

"Tell that to your wife," Roger said. "There were no negotiations there." Ten glared at him. Roger raised his hands. "Just making a point. I didn't mean anything."

"Maybe that was one insider making the decision. It's hard for me to believe that was handed down by the president."

"Isn't that enough?" Jacob asked. "How do we stop that from happening again?"

"Local police," Ten said.

Jacob stretched his legs out and looked away. "And all the newspapers and television stations."

"Exactly." Ten leaned forward.

Maria looked into her lap. "It could backfire."

"Anything we do could backfire. You said it yourself—we've been lucky so far. Well, that luck can't keep coming. Something has to change. We have to throw a monkey wrench into the works. Get them scrambling."

"Maybe," Jacob said.

"We'll stop running," Roger said.

Maria pushed her fingers through her hair. "I just want it over with. I'm in."

Roger nodded slowly. "In."

Jacob cocked his head. "How do we get to the local police while we're holed up in these woods?"

"After dark," Ten said.

"What if those guys catch us?" Roger asked.

"They're probably long gone. Probably packed up our stuff too. They don't want to get caught either, whoever they are." Ten waited for a comment and when none came, he turned toward the woods and started to get up. "It's almost dark; I'm going exploring."

"Not without all of us," Maria said. She pushed up and stood beside him. "You good for now?" she asked Roger.

"Good enough," he said.

Ten saw him wince while Jacob helped him up, but Roger sucked it up pretty quickly and pushed away from Jacob to walk on his own. Ten approved of Roger's tenacity. His side still hurt, so Roger's must be worse.

"You can get us back to here, if we're going deeper into the forest?" Roger asked.

"I can do that," Ten said, "but I doubt we'll have to. There must be other buildings around here and we'll run into them if we walk far enough. That's my guess."

By the time they came upon another road, it was dark. They stopped to think things through. "Four people walking along the side of the road isn't going to look normal," Ten said. "How about only one of us remains in plain view, while the others stay inside the woods. Anyone slow down or stop, and everyone ducks except the one on the road until we find out the situation."

Jacob shrugged. "Makes sense to me."

Ten glanced around. Everyone seemed to agree, so he went on. "Who's going to be exposed?"

"Any one of us could be recognized by the right person," Jacob said. "Except that you and Maria are east coasters. Maybe you'd be less likely to be recognized. Either of you willing?"

"I'll do it," Maria said. "It'll be easier for me to walk too." She turned toward Roger. "Unless you'd rather take the easy walk."

"I'm good," he said.

"Someone might be more likely to stop for a woman," Jacob said. "We could get a ride to the police station, ask to be placed in protective custody."

"Any idea where we are?" Ten asked.

"Near Portland?" Roger guessed.

"Let's find a sign or two," Jacob said. "I've been all around here. I just need a mark."

They agreed and Maria started walking along the road, while the others maintained a safe distance into the woods. The going wasn't the best, but they continued to talk with Maria so she didn't get too far ahead of them.

It didn't take long and a Ford Focus slowed up ahead, stopped, then began to back up.

"I'm getting closer. You two hunker down." Ten crouched and ran for the edge of the road, then ducked behind a tree at the last minute. "I'm right here," he whispered loudly to Maria.

"Good," she said. "I don't know what to do."

"Play it by ear," Ten said. "You can handle it."

The car pulled to a stop near Maria, and she walked to the passenger side window, which came down as she approached.

"Didn't see a car broke down. Where you headed?"

"What's the next town?" Maria asked.

"Going toward Clackamas," the man said. "You from around here?"

"No. It's a long story. Look, I have friends," Maria said, but let the sentence go at that point.

"With you, or friends you're going to see?"

"With me. Yes."

"Bring 'em. I got room." Suddenly the man's voice sounded a bit nervous, and who wouldn't be, Ten thought. A strange woman walking along the road at night… with friends hiding in the woods. The man probably wished he hadn't stopped in the first place. But something kept him there, something stopped him from flooring it and getting the hell out of there.

Ten walked from behind the tree and jumped the ditch to get to the road.

"Your boyfriend?" the man asked.

Maria shook her head. "Just a friend," she said.

Ten wondered if that made the man more nervous or less nervous, but didn't wait to find out. "I'll sit up front," Ten said.

Maria waved him away. "No, you won't; I will. He trusted me."

"What's going on?" the man asked.

Maria opened the front door and sat down. She kept the door open and put only one leg into the car. "There's more," she said. "I told you I had friends."

Ten opened a back door and slid all the way over against the far door. The car smelled fresh, not like some of the junk heaps they'd stolen along the way. "It's okay. We're safe. Really," he said, but then thought that might not actually convince the man but do just the opposite.

The driver didn't answer. He held the steering wheel with both hands.

Jacob helped Roger into the car, then slid in next to him and shut the door.

"You okay going to Clackamas?" the man asked.

"We're going to the police station," Maria said.

"Don't know where that is," the man said.

Maria took over the conversation. "What's your name?"

"Chet."

"We're being chased by some people, Chet. Well, not chased. We escaped. We need to get to the police. We suspect that's our best option at this point."

He appeared to ease up, knowing that they weren't criminals. "Maybe if we find an officer along the way," he said.

"How about Portland," Jacob said from the back seat. "The Portland police?"

"Twenty minutes," Chet said.

"Would you mind?" Maria said. "We really need the help."

"No. No, I don't mind. The police station in Portland."

"And do you have a cell phone? We'd like to call the paper," she said.

"Or the local TV news station," Jacob said.

Chet pulled a smart phone from his pocket, messed with it somehow that Ten couldn't see, and handed it to Maria.

"What's local news around here?" She held up the phone.

"Channel Four News," Chet said.

Maria called. "I have breaking news," she said into the phone.

Chapter 29

"We need to get to the television news station, not the police. Not yet," Maria said. "This will break everything open if they believe us. The police would check our story and could easily be intercepted by ISTI." She turned to look at Ten sitting behind Chet. "The guy on the phone didn't sound too convinced that I was who I said I was."

"So what if he checks us out and we're met by ISTI?" Jacob asked. "We have the same problem."

"Who's ISTI?" Chet asked.

"International Security for Technological Innovations," Ten answered.

"The government?" Chet questioned. "You escaped from the government?"

"They tried to get rid of us, to protect the country from what we knew, from the research we've been doing for the past seven years. Only a few of us escaped. At least, that's what we assume."

"The government is looking for you?" Chet repeated with a nervous twitch. He white-knuckled the steering wheel and sped up, as though that would get them there faster and get him off the hook sooner. "You don't have to tell them I helped."

Maria put a hand on his shoulder. "You can go as soon as you drop us off. No one will know unless you tell them."

"Thank you." His shoulders appeared to relax and he rotated his hands over the steering wheel as though greasing it with his palms.

"Then we have twenty minutes," Roger said. He lifted a bloody hand. "My side feels better. Either that or it's numb."

"We'll get you fixed up as soon as we can," Ten said.

"What's wrong with him?" Chet asked.

"Shot," Ten and Maria said at the same time.

"Scratched!" Roger yelled into the front seat. "I don't like the idea that I was shot."

"How's this story go when we get there?" Jacob said after a few minutes of silence.

"The truth," Ten said. "Maria already told them who she was, that we're involved in something top secret, and that we want to expose a government activity that we feel the public should know about. We're whistleblowers. We may have to leave the country."

"Not after this," Jacob said. "We will be taken into custody though. You know that. We'll probably have to stand trial."

"Not without everyone on my list standing trial," Ten said.

Jacob smiled. "I forgot about your list." He cocked his head and leaned around Roger to look at Ten. "Maybe we negotiate."

"Maybe we do," Ten said.

"Do you mind if I ask what the big deal is?" Chet said.

"Better you don't know just yet," Jacob said.

Maria turned in her seat. "Why not? He's trusted us this far. Why not tell him. It won't matter in a few minutes anyway."

"Then?" Chet said.

She looked at him, then back at the others again.

Jacob shrugged. Ten said, "Sure, why not."

Maria explained who they were and what they'd discovered. It didn't take long. She gave him the short version, and why it was so important that no government have the capability to use the technology the four of them were involved with.

"I'm in a car full of geniuses," Chet said.

Ten wondered if that's all he got out of the explanation.

"This is important to everyone," Chet said under his breath, and Ten knew what Maria had told him was sinking in, that Chet let it roll around in his head until he got it. He even started to nod as he thought. Ten felt that was a good sign. "We'll take a bit of a roundabout way," Chet said, "just in case there's someone there to pick you up before you're inside." He turned his head toward Maria. "Thanks for telling me the truth. I'll get you to the back door safely. I doubt they'll expect that. From there, you're on your own."

"I knew you'd understand."

Jacob pulled the thumb drive out of his pocket. "Take this." He handed it over the front seat.

"You sure that's a good idea?" Ten asked.

"If we don't get on the news for some reason, create a file about what Maria told you, and upload it to this thumb drive. Make a dozen copies and sent one to every television station and newspaper you can. Keep sending it until someone listens. Can you do that?"

"I promise." Chet took the drive and shoved it into his shirt pocket.

"This might put you in danger," Ten said. "It's a huge responsibility."

"I can mail them from all over the place. No one will ever find out." He looked into the rearview mirror and leaned to the side so that he could see Ten. "This is important." He appeared to understand.

Ten reached for his side and noticed how little pain was left. He touched his shoulder where his first close call with being shot occurred. He thought back to Amy, Groucho, and his unborn child. Everything was winding down. This was it. Either they were caught by ISTI officials and no one ever hears about them again, or they're on the news and all hell broke loose. Maybe they're dead and Chet spreads the word. There were a lot of options now. More than when they started. He could hardly remember how they'd gotten where they were. Four of them, assembled along the way. One man killed trying to save them. The costs were too high. And some of the decision makers were still alive. He glanced out the window at the darkness. It was almost over and he wondered if they'd won or failed. It was too early to tell, but he wanted to know. He wanted it to end, to finally be over.

They drove into a more populated area. The station couldn't be far now. No one ever asked how Chet knew where the station was, or how he even knew the streets downtown so well. They had turned their lives over to a stranger in a car.

Ten shook his head at how ludicrous the situation appeared, how lucky they'd all been, the four of them, and wondered how much longer that luck was going to stick.

"Two blocks," Chet said. "I'll drop you off out back. The door is most likely locked and you'll have to rattle it to get in."

"Or shoot the lock." Ten lifted his pistol.

"Holy shit," Chet said. "I didn't know you had guns."

"You do now," Ten said. "We'll get inside."

Chet pulled up near the back door. A tiny plaque indicated that it was indeed Channel 4 News. Everyone jumped out. Maria leaned in and patted Chet's hand. "Thank you." She stepped out of the car.

"I know what to do if I don't see you on the news," Chet said. "Trust me."

"You're all we got," Ten said. He turned around, walked up to the door, checked to be sure it was locked, then shot the lock and shoved open the door. They stepped inside what looked like a break room. One person had started to get up, probably after hearing the lock get blasted off. She stood.

Her chair lay behind her. But she stood still, as though she thought that by not moving no one could see her. Well, they could.

"We called in with breaking news," Ten said. The woman, dressed casually in dark gray slacks and a blue-gray blouse, stared at the gun. Ten pushed the pistol into his pants and held up his hands. "Really, we need your help."

"Who'd you talk to?" the woman asked.

Maria stepped forward. "Some guy at the news desk." The woman didn't say anything and moved slowly. "We're serious," Maria said. "Where is he?"

The woman rushed toward the door. The others followed, Ten bringing up the rear. As soon as the woman entered a larger room with multiple desks, a young man stood. There were only two others in the room. "You're the scientists?" he exclaimed.

"Exactly," Maria said. The man looked shocked that they were there. "You didn't believe me?" Maria asked.

"I was checking what you said on the phone. Tempest Nesbit was supposed to be dead. Which one—?"

Ten came around from behind. "That would be me."

The man bent to look at his computer and then look up at Ten. He shook his head. "Holy shit."

"You said it, chief," Jacob said. "Now, where are the cameras?"

"Wait here, I'll go into the studio." He took off and Jacob followed him. Ten, Roger, and Maria waited with the other two employees, one behind a desk and the woman who had led them into the room.

"You're for real," the woman said, her eyes wide. "Frank told me about you. We thought it was a crank call."

"We're not cranks," Ten said.

The woman finally must have noticed Roger holding his bloody shirt and screeched. "You're hurt!" She rushed to his side.

"I wrapped it the best I could with what we had," Maria said.

"I can take care of this." The woman led Roger over to a desk and helped him sit down. "Wait here and I'll get the first aid kit." She disappeared back into the kitchen.

When Ten turned back around, Jacob and Frank were coming back into the room. "We're ready for you," Frank said.

"And ISTI is on its way," Jacob said. He looked over at Frank and shrugged.

"I had no idea," Frank said. "But now that I do, let's get you on the air."

Chapter 30

They were led into a side room near the main studio. A cameraman held cables and appeared to be setting up. Another kid rolled in some sound equipment.

Ten shook his head. "What's going on?"

"We're setting up to tape you; why?" Frank said.

"We need to go live," Ten said. "If anyone from ISTI shows up, they'll confiscate this recording and nothing will get out. We'll all be dead meat."

"This is how we do it," Frank said. "We'll get a reporter in here and interview you. It'll be our lead story on the eleven o'clock news."

"Now!" Ten yelled. "You can't wait for this."

The cameraman, a burly guy with big hands, removed his headphones and looked over at Ten.

Ten pulled his pistol. "You people don't scare me. This is too important. If you checked on us, they're on their way. You can't do this. Not now. We're putting our necks on the line." Maria reached for him, but Ten pulled away. "This is our only chance."

"There's Chet," Jacob said matter-of-factly.

"I have the list," Ten said, "not Chet."

All this time Frank, the sound man, and the cameraman stared at him. "I can't do a live feed without permission," Frank said.

Jacob turned to Frank, then back toward Ten. "You're right." He looked at Maria. "Now's our only chance." To

Frank, he said, "Make an executive decision or you're going to have blood on your hands."

"You're going to shoot me?" Frank stepped back toward the door.

"No, you idiot; ours. They're going to come in here and finish what they started. They're going to make us go away. You saw the information about Ten. No one will even know we were here."

Beads of sweat appeared on Frank's upper lip and forehead. The cameraman said, "Live feed it is." Frank looked right at him. "Create a breaking news segment," the cameraman said. Frank nodded and walked out of the room. "Let's go," the cameraman said.

"Thank you," Ten said.

"Worse case is they fire me, right?" the cameraman said. "But this sounds serious. Especially with you holding that gun."

"Sorry. I didn't mean anything."

A few moments later, a young woman, dressed smartly in a green skirt and blouse and green pumps, rushed into the room. She had shoulder-length brown hair. She held out her hand. "I'm Karen Burroway."

Ten came over and shook Karen's hand after handing the gun to Maria.

"Can you tell me a little bit about why you're here?" she said right away. "I like to have some information so I can ask questions."

Ten smiled broadly. He wanted to hug her, but instead, he told her briefly what Maria had told Frank. "Frank didn't clue you in?"

"He was probably checking your information," she said, as though proper procedures were important even for such breaking news. "We don't want to look stupid. But he said this is legit, so we're ready to roll." She motioned for Jacob and Maria to stand near her and Ten, then turned toward the camera.

Frank came into the room and closed the door. A little red light above the door blinked a few times and then turned green. Frank pointed at Karen.

"I'm Karen Burroway with a Channel 4 News special report…"

* * *

"Unbelievable," Karen said. "And you say you know how to stop it?"

"Wasn't that hard to figure out once we had room to test it," Jacob said. He stood a foot above Karen.

As soon as they opened the sound-room door, they could hear phones ringing in the other room. When they walked into the main studio, Roger was standing with three men in dark suits. "Here we go," Maria said.

Ten pushed past her and stood front and center. "Not quite."

"You're all coming with us," one of the men said. Then he looked at Karen, then past Ten. "Is that on?"

Ten turned to see the cameraman in the doorway. The big man nodded to the man in the suit's question. Ten had to smile. He was beginning to really like the cameraman. Frank, on the other hand, stood off to the side and looked as though he was actually shaking in his shoes. So that's where the saying comes from, Ten thought.

"Turn it off," the man said.

The cameraman shook his head. More phones were ringing from the other room.

Karen rushed forward so that she could hold her microphone between Ten and the man in the suit.

Ten stepped closer. "As I mentioned on the air a few moments ago, I have a list of the scientists involved in this research as well as the six men who okayed the killing of us and our families. You may want to know that I read that list off."

Karen said, "We've already pushed this story out to every independent station we could. You can't stop this now." She had a defiant look in her eyes. "You can't get away with something like this," she said. "I don't care what government you work for."

"What do you want?" the man asked Ten.

"Impunity," Ten said. "For the four of us, and any of the other scientists who happen to still be alive." He lowered his head, then brought his chin up and said, "And penalty to those who approved these murders."

"We can't guarantee anything like that. We're only—"

"Then get someone on the phone who can," Ten said.

The man talking to Ten shrugged.

"The president," Jacob said as he stepped closer to Ten and leaned toward Karen's microphone.

"You taping or are we live?" the man asked.

"Live as can be," Karen said. Even Ten couldn't tell if she was bluffing or not.

"It takes time to reach the president," the man said.

"We can wait," Ten said.

"This is live?" the man asked again.

"You bet," Karen answered again.

The man in the suit looked unhappy. He turned toward his two buddies, the ones who flanked Roger, but neither of them made a sound or a move of any kind. They were statues.

"Come up with a plan," Ten said.

From the doorway into the other room, where the ringing phones were, stepped the other young man who was sitting at a desk earlier. He cleared his throat. "No need for a plan," he said. "The president is on the line."

"Really?" Karen said as a big smile crossed her face. This must have been the biggest news story she'd ever been involved with.

Ten noticed that from the back of the main studio, several well-dressed men and women entered the room.

"Can we patch him through?" Karen asked.

The sound man went to work right away. "Have it online in three minutes," he said.

Ten cocked his head toward the men in front of him, then turned to look at Jacob and Maria. "Looks like it's almost over."

Maria put her hand on Ten's shoulder and stepped closer to him. "What about your original plan?" She wasn't being snide about what he had originally set out to do, but seemed like she actually wanted to know.

It took Ten a moment to let her question sink in. He took a deep breath. He no longer felt the need to kill anyone else. He felt relief unlike any he'd ever felt. Maybe that's how Maria felt, maybe that's what she wanted. It felt good.

"I suppose I can let the law take over. Those men will get what they deserve."

Maria smiled at him. "Yes, they will."

The sound man yelled from across the room. "President on the air in three, two…"

THE END

Author's Note

Now is the time. Please review this book. Authors depend on readers like you to help promote their works. If you enjoyed this book, please recommend it to others, as well. Thank you.

—Terry

About the Author

Terry Persun has been writing and publishing poetry, short stories, and novels since the early 1970s. He has been the recipient of many novel and poetry awards over the years, including the Star of Washington Award, a Silver IPPY for historical fiction, two Book of the Year finalist awards in the science fiction category, two finalist awards from the USA Book News International Book Awards (one in science fiction and one in historical fiction), two poetry chapbook awards, and a Jeanne Voge Poetry Award. Terry writes in a variety of genres, including science fiction, thriller, mystery, and mainstream fiction. His Doublesight novels were selected as a Kindle World for fan-fiction writers. He is a respected keynoter and speaker at libraries, writers' groups, writers' conferences, and universities across the country. Terry has an MA in creative writing from SUNY Stony Brook.

For More News About Terry Persun,
Signup For Our Newsletter:

http://wbp.bz/newsletter

Word-of-mouth is critical to an author's long-
term success. If you appreciated this book please
leave a review on the Amazon sales page:

http://wbp.bz/killingmachinea